# PEKUTU

## A PRINCE AT WAR

# C. J. NEYLON

TINY TREE
CHILDREN'S BOOKS

First Published 2022
Tiny Tree Children's Books
(an imprint of Matthew James Publishing Ltd)
Unit 46, Goyt Mill
Marple
Stockport
SK6 7HX

www.tinytreebooks.com

ISBN: 978-1-913230-53-1

# Contents

## PART I
## Boyhood

## PART II
## Training

# PART III
# Resistance

# PART I
# Boyhood

# Chapter 1

It came as a deep and joyful surprise. As soon as Peredis, with his tutor Adhemar, cleared the lip of the crater and saw the citadel of Eremore rising majestically above the ocean, he realised something was different. This time, he wasn't returning as a stranger. His very being had soaked into those granite pinnacles, towers and terraces where colourful flags and banners proclaimed a different order, a realm where he, too, now belonged.

His friend Anton, of course, had been born and bred here, and loved to show him the secret paths and cuts which criss-crossed the cobbled streets and alleys of the city, places he had explored since his childhood. The higher you climbed in that great pyramid of stone, the narrower and more dangerous the way became, until you clung to a narrow ledge surrounding the topmost pinnacle, where a solitary bell hung for sounding in an emergency.

It had rung only once in a thousand years, Anton said as he settled them into a niche where they could both sit comfortably and look out over the harbour to the open sea.

"What's the point of a bell you never ring?" Peredis asked, laughing.

"The bell summons us to war," Anton said, after a long pause. "If that day ever comes, which is very rare. The last time it rang for the uprising led by your father."

"I saw him leave Heimhaven with the militia," Peredis said mournfully. "I was standing on the Chieftain's terrace with my mother and we watched them all marching off together. But within moments my mother turned away and went indoors."

"Why?"

"Because she knew, I think. Somehow she knew it was the last time."

"And he never returned."

"I never saw him alive again. He came home in a funeral boat and was buried in Heimhaven."

"Did you miss him?"

"Yes, I did. I went everywhere with him when I was a young lad. He taught me to fish in the ocean."

"That sounds fun."

"Oh, it was." He had a sudden vision of that long forgotten past and had to look away from his friend with salt stinging his eyes.

"My father and mother live in a village along the coast," Anton said, his mind elsewhere. He hadn't noticed his friend's distress. "I don't get to see them much."

"You should see them while you still can," Peredis said, recovering himself and then remembered ... "Ah, of course, your parents won't ever die, will they?"

"Not as long as they stay in Eremore, no."

Peredis still found it hard to understand this immortal gift of the Eremoreans. When you walked the streets among them, the people seemed to be of flesh and blood like normal humans. But at the same time they were different. They had a certain elegance, a willowiness which was very attractive, and they looked at you with eyes of glittering topaz blue and smiled quietly in a way that suggested they knew something you couldn't possibly know. They never shouted or raised their voices, and their speech was musical and gentle.

Was he really one of them? He had to ask himself. Looking back, he saw an arrogant and difficult young man, not at all like these gentle, civilised people with their dignified manners. But he had learned important lessons during his time in the citadel, and he was blessed in having Anton always at his side, checking his behaviour with a whispered word and a restraining hand.

To others, Peredis gave the impression that he was afraid of nothing and nobody, but that wasn't true. Whenever he passed close by and the Chancellor's stone grey eyes held him in their grip, he felt a chill around that stern figure and a tremor passed through him. He was all the more nervous because of a conversation he'd had with Adhemar on their return from La Motte. His tutor had told him that if he wanted to know more about his own history, he would need to explore the Annals in the citadel library. His heart sank. He knew this meant approaching Chancellor Gryss, a prospect he didn't look forward to. So it was with some trepidation that he went to find Gryss in his office in the southern wing of the palace. What struck him when he went in was the sheer bareness of the room. The desk, though large, had only two sheets of paper on it, with the remaining surface completely uncluttered. Shelves lined the walls neatly arranged with labelled boxes in rigorous order.

"Well?" Gryss asked, looking up from his task and putting down his pen.

"I believe you are the author of the Annals, sir," Peredis began hesitantly, always at the mercy of that stony gaze.

"That is one of my duties, yes."

"Anton has shown me the Annals gallery above the library and I've tried to find some record of my birth and family ..." He paused, hoping the Chancellor would make this easy for him. But he didn't.

"Yes?" was all he said.

"But I found no mention of my mother, my father or myself."

"No," he uttered without any expression. "That is so."

"I wondered if you could help me." Irritated by his attitude, Peredis started to feel bolder. "I should be grateful for your help."

There was a long silence, then he said, "So I take it you want to read the Pages of Shame ..."

The strength of the words took him completely by surprise and left him speechless. Strangely, he felt himself blushing as if caught out in something indecent.

"The Pages of Shame," Gryss repeated. " Are you sure that is what you want?"

"Yes, sir," he recovered enough to say, "if it's where I will find my own history."

"Officially they're called the Red Annals. You will require a key," Gryss said, opening a drawer in his desk and taking out a keyring. "The Red Annals are found on the upper library landing, through a door, not to the right but to the left of the stairs. Unlike the public Annals, these records are arranged alphabetically, so you will have no trouble finding what you want. The pages you seek will have a red border, designating their sensitivity."

He reached across to hand over the key. "Once in the room, close and lock the door behind you. Do not leave the door open at any time. Bring the key straight back to me when you have finished for the day. And remember ..."

Peredis stopped and waited as he turned away.

"Go alone, not with your friend, and never speak of what you read there. You are not to copy or repeat anything you see in the Red Annals. They are not for publication in any form. Do you understand?"

"I understand."

But the truth was, the young man didn't understand at all. He had no idea where his quest would take him and, given the severity of the Chancellor's words, he was quite scared as to what he might find.

With the steep winding ascent of the library stairs, his heart began thumping furiously as he arrived on the uppermost landing. Hidden in the shadows to the left was a door he hadn't noticed when he came with Anton. The key fitted and turned silently as if in a well-oiled lock, and the door slid sideways on a groove without a sound.

Peredis entered the room nervously, almost on tiptoe, like a thief, as if he had no business in the place. He used the key to close and lock the door behind him.

Now he found himself alone in a darkened gallery with a single desk at the near end with a reading lamp lit above it. This room was smaller than the other Annals library and had no windows, only a wall light at the end of each stack. Peredis started to search along the shelves tracing the letters on the red bindings with his finger and before long found the alphabetical order the Chancellor had mentioned. Soon he was able to follow the sequence of shelves which took him to D, then to the volume DO–DU. He grasped the heavy leather-bound tome in both hands and carried it to the reading desk to inspect his find. It turned out to hold handwritten pages with the topic of each section written large on an opening sheet. It was a matter of moments to find 'Doromea', the search helped by the red edge bordering the pages under her name as Gryss had said. His hands trembled as he turned the first title page and studied the text that followed. It was written on weighted paper in clean copy, neatly and clearly penned in black ink with no corrections or alterations.

*Here we must speak of Princess Doromea, and of the events that brought her low and brought shame on her name.*

*It is customary that marriages in Eremore are arranged by the families concerned and it so happened that, from her childhood, Princess Doromea was betrothed to Stephane, the only son of Chancellor Gryss.*

He had to stop reading. Suddenly it was as if a veil dropped and everything that had happened to his parents was bathed in a new light. Of course, it was clear to him now, and he understood for the first time, why the Chancellor felt so aggrieved and severe towards his mother Doromea.

*This betrothal was broken by Doromea's decision to follow her heart rather than the arranged custom, and thereby the union of the two families became impossible.*

*Doromea chose to join herself to the mortal world of humans, passing through the gateway to what the Eremoreans call the Outside. When one goes through that gateway, one must leave Eremorean customs behind and enter the world of humans. However, to cross over into the mortal world, to form a union with a human, brings with it a sacrifice, a price which Doromea had not foreseen. As an Eremorean princess, she thought she could love her man, bear his children, and travel back and forth between the two worlds as a couple. But it was not to be.*

*What she failed to understand was the terrible legacy which had originally created the ancient division between Eremore and humankind. In pre-historic times, what we call the Time of Bliss, all of nature lived together in peace and harmony. For reasons we cannot understand, humans brought death to creation, and as a result our people had to retreat from the earth to a safe domain. Protection was raised all around and the gateways closed. A shield covered us both from sky and sea.*

*It may be asked, then, how Doromea came to have an encounter in the Outside. In fact, her meeting with the man Aenvar Egilsson took place in a borderland between the two worlds where she used to go for her own entertainment, always accompanied by courtiers. But it seems she enjoyed the adventure of losing her companions and riding through the forest in a reckless manner which could only lead to danger. So it was that she came upon the man Aenvar Egilsson, and soon afterwards, blindly following her emotions, she gave him a token of silver, believing this would open the gateway for her lover, but she was mistaken. The Eremore court would not allow it. Because of Aenvar's humanity, the gateway would always remain closed to him. Knowing this, Doromea chose to follow the man into his* nation, leaving Eremore behind. At the same time she herself became mortal. Her love obliged her to embrace death. Naturally this outcome was known from the very start, for Aenvar's death was already written in the Annals of the Future.

The laws of Eremore are not heartless and through the intercession of king Odolf certain provision had been made which softened the court's judgement. It was permitted that after Aenvar's death, Doromea would recover the right to return to Eremore, a right which she invoked only for the purpose of presenting her son Peredis for royal adoption by the king. At that ceremony, the king gave his adopted son a silver dagger with special powers.

It is important for the record to state, as well, that the man Aenvar Egilsson was a renowned warrior with a long ancestry. For this reason, his character was initially held in great suspicion by our people, who are not of warlike culture. But as the surrounding threat of Europus grew more and more significant, it was seen as vital to send our own forces in alliance with those of the Visionaries led by Aenvar, in their battle for freedom across the old continent. A whole contingent of heroic volunteers of Eremore sacrificed their lives in that campaign.

Peredis stopped in amazement, and with his index finger went back and retraced the whole passage he had just read, words which threw even more new light on the story. He was suddenly confused and lost for understanding. How could it be true? Had his mother joined her life to Aenvar knowing in advance of his inevitable death? But surely, even then, she would have chosen to return after he died. Why hadn't she gone back to her own people? Peredis read on:

*Following the battle of the Peak of Larroun in which Aenvar lost his life, King Odolf sent messengers to Doromea calling her back to Eremore but she was unwilling to go and this refusal caused her father great sorrow. She never explained her reasons but to some it was clear that she could not face the shame of returning. Others said she believed that only in death could she be reunited with her lover, and this meant more to her than any other bond.*

None of this gave Peredis any comfort. He turned away from the pages, feeling an acute pain of loss, as well as an anguished sense that the shame she couldn't face was his own, too. In these pages, he had learned beyond doubt that not all Eremoreans viewed his parents with pride or honour, and the Chancellor's family least of all. And also the sheer extent of his mother's sacrifice for Aenvar had been revealed for the first time.

But this wasn't yet the whole story. He needed to find the account of his adoption by the king and it seemed that in these pages, at least, there was no further mention of that event. He went back to the stacks and searched for the volume P. It took longer to find but in due course he extracted the tome PA– PE and carried it to the reading desk. His heart was pounding again as he flicked through the pages and finally came across the section titled with his own name, Peredis Aenvarsson. Here there were no red borders, which gave him some encouragement, but he was still nervous as to what he would find. He turned the title page and started to read:

*By virtue of descent through his mother, Princess Doromea, Peredis was of Eremorean blood and related to the royal family. He therefore had privileges in his own right and freedom to come and go from Eremore. However such rights and privileges had to be granted him through ancient ceremony, and with this aim Doromea was able to bring her eight year old son into the realm and present him to King Odolf for the formal crossing of hands. Henceforth Peredis would enjoy the protection of the king as his adopted father and would be summoned to court at the age of sixteen for his studies and preparation for manhood.*

*The king, out of his love for Doromea, promised to do everything in his power to further the boy's development. To this end it was arranged for the gate-watcher, Adhemar de la Brèche, to act as tutor for the boy until his sixteenth birthday.*

*For further on this topic see the Annals of the Future.*

The Annals of the Future? What was it that Adhemar had said to him? "Perhaps you will be honoured more for your future than for your past."

So where would he find the Annals of the Future to discover more? Would they be filed away on some other hidden floor of the library?

That was his question for the Chancellor when he returned the key to him.

In reply Gryss gave a sardonic smile. "The Annals of the Future remain to be written," he said. "There is no key to open them."

"How am I to see them, then?" Peredis asked a little impatiently, "As it says in the volume about me."

"How to read your future? You must find the hand that writes."

"That's what Adhemar said to me about the Annals and the history and that's why I came to you. Is it you? Do you write the future as well?" Peredis was beginning to sound rather frustrated.

"Whose hand can write the future until it is past?" He opened the desk drawer to put away the key. "I take it you don't need this any more?"

"That doesn't make sense," Peredis protested. "Whose hand? I don't understand."

"Perhaps the king can tell you more. He is your guardian, after all."

Peredis abruptly left the Chancellor's office with less grace than usual and went out on to the great terrace of the palace overlooking the sea. He needed to be alone. Why did he feel the Chancellor was just playing with him? Everything he said was couched in mystery. Nothing was plain and simple. It was true that he felt a certain guilt for not having dared to ask him about his son, Stephane, betrothed to his mother Doromea and abandoned by her. What had become of him? Perhaps Anton could explain more later.

Still, for now this unknown future was starting to fill his thoughts. He needed to find the signs that would guide him to the Annals of the Future, wherever they were to be found. The words "All will be well" came into his mind and for a moment he forgot where they came from. "All will be well ..." They were his mother's words as she pressed the silver box into his hand, the same little box that he carried always in his pocket, just as he always carried Odolf's silver dagger on his belt. He recalled the other words of that final conversation. "One day," she said, "this token will bring you your dream, and my salvation, too. For the one who holds this token will redeem me from my fate..."

He understood now. Her fate was the shame that had surrounded her at the end of her life. It was all too clear. How could she possibly have returned to live in the palace alongside the grim and unforgiving figure of the Chancellor?

At the same time Peredis began to see something more. He saw beyond her shame to what would be written in the Annals of the Future, leading to what she called his dream, and the possibility of redemption.

And whose hand would write the Annals of the Future? His own hand, of course. He would write his future with his own hand. The Annals of the Future would take Peredis to his dream, and the silver token would go to the one who would redeem her.

# Chapter 2

"Where have you been? I've been looking all over for you." Anton appeared in the doorway of the great terrace.

Peredis felt bad about not telling him, but remembered Gryss's stern words. "I was just looking around the library."

"I went up there, and looked in at the Annals as well. No sign of you."

"Oh, I was probably looking around one of those stacks where there isn't much light. You probably just didn't see me."

"I called out."

"Sorry, Anton, I didn't hear you."

His friend shrugged. "No matter. Anyway, I was coming to tell you they've hung the new tapestry, the one they've been working on for ages. It tells the story of the last battle of Larroun. Everyone's there admiring it. Do you want to see it?"

"Absolutely," Peredis said excitedly, "Let's go."

Anton paused a moment. "But do you really want to see? I only ask because your father's shown in it, you know." He took his friend's arm and held it gently.

"Yes," came the firm reply. "Before I wasn't, but now I'm sure."

It was true. He didn't know what to expect and Anton was right to warn his friend in advance. As they entered the tapestry room they saw a crowd of courtiers and others standing around. They didn't get a good view until they were right in front of it. Then Peredis stepped back in horror.

The first impact was stunning, from the sheer force and colour of the work. You have to imagine a huge picture of warfare, a struggling chaotic mass of men and weapons, the wounded fallen or staggering, barely upright, blood on the ground, flags tattered and almost destroyed, smoke and darkness overhead.

Peredis hadn't taken in the whole picture, it was too large, but then he saw it: the axe, the fourfold axe lying on the bloodstained grass of the hillside, the shining symbol of his father's authority. He was shocked to see it so vividly, dropped and abandoned. Then he saw the whole picture. His father, turned half away so his face was only in profile, was down on one knee, his arm raised as if to protect himself. Beside him another figure bent to shield him and hold him up.

"I know him," Peredis cried hoarsely. "I know him from Heimhaven. It's Gorka, look, he's trying to help my father."

But you could see the effort was useless and there was blood and anguish on Gorka's face as he desperately tried to support Aenvar. Then the smell overcame everything ...

*The smell is unbearable, its poison fills Peredis' lungs with caustic and sulphurous fumes. As it chokes him, he feels a dreadful sense of being engulfed and seized, and there's a penetrating sense of evil and horror. Something truly gruesome invades him, like being pulled directly into the ghastly writhing mass of the picture. He can see the bloody combat at close quarters, hear the agonised cries of the suffering. He tries to cover his ears, his eyes, but there's no escape, no relief, and he can't even turn away because the picture has him in its hold. There's a roaring in his ears. Then blackness engulfs him and he is falling to the floor. He feels Anton trying to catch him, just as Gorka is trying to hold up his father.*

*Then out of the surrounding darkness there looms a horrendous figure armed to the teeth, a ghostly image not of life, but of death. Peredis is more than scared. He's terrified ...*

*** 

Peredis had no idea how long he was unconscious. When at last he woke, the first face he saw was that of his tutor Adhemar.

"Where am I?" he asked, looking around.

"You're in Eremore, in the king's apartments. Relax, my boy, you're safe and well. You just need to rest."

At the same moment, Anton came into the room and gave a great sigh of relief as he saw his friend awake. "How is he? Has he spoken yet?"

"He's just woken, this very minute. We must be patient."

"Will he recover?"

"When he's strong enough I'll take him back to La Motte, his uncle Robert's estate in the mountains."

"Can he talk? Can he say what happened to him?"

"It's too soon to ask questions. We'll let him tell his story in his own time. In the meantime, we must keep an eye on him." Adhemar lowered his voice. "All I know is that something bad happened. Something that tried to overcome him. It has to do with the tapestry, the scene of his father Aenvar's death."

"I did ask him if he really wanted to see it," Anton said. "I feel so guilty now. I should have realised it was too much for him to bear."

"You're not to blame, Anton, not in the least. The king is concerned for him, by the way. He wants to be told when Peredis is able to sit up and have a visit from him. Will you take a message?"

"Of course," Anton said. Left with Peredis on his own, Adhemar came and sat beside the bed.

"We'll return to La Motte as soon as you're fit and well, in a day or two," he smiled. Peredis nodded, half closing his eyes. "I'd like that," he said. It was clear he still felt bewildered and confused but the thought of returning to his childhood home made him feel secure.

A knock sounded on the door, announcing a visit from the king. His concern was natural since following the death of Peredis' mother, King Odolf had adopted him as his son.

Adhemar greeted the king as he entered. "He's still rather shaky," he said. "And not really up for conversation."

"No matter," Odolf said, crossing to the bedside and taking the boy's hand. "I can see he's on the mend. That's the most important thing."

"Thank you for coming to see me," Peredis said quietly.

"What's the plan?" the king asked, turning to Adhemar.

"I'm taking him to La Motte as soon as we can travel. A little rest and recuperation is just what's needed."

"You're right," said the king. "Take your time, avoid stress and enjoy the mountain air. You can spend time as well as helping Robert on the estate, very therapeutic! So go with our blessing."

# Chapter 3

As they rode up to the house in its quiet valley, it was hard to tell which welcome was more enthusiastic, that of Uncle Robert, who was not really an uncle but a dear friend of Peredis' father, Aenvar, or the bounding delight of Orlando and Oliver, the two hunting dogs who accompanied their master everywhere.

Peredis gave a deep sigh of contentment, breathing in the fresh mountain air and absorbing the peace and tranquillity of the place he loved and called home.

Adhemar put an arm around the young man's shoulders. "You'll soon feel better here," he said in a comforting voice.

He was aware that Peredis was still damaged, deep inside himself. The wound had come from somewhere in his depths and would take time to heal.

As he played with the dogs, Robert and Adhemar watched him. "Tell me more about how this all came about." Robert asked as they made their way indoors.

"It's very strange," Adhemar said. "All I know is that it comes from a place of evil. That's why we must keep protection around the boy. Evil happened on the Peak of Larroun and left its stamp on the very earth," he said ominously.

"Who said that?" asked Robert, curious.

"Someone with dark power," replied Adhemar, and said no more.

# Chapter 4

"Robert has something to show you," Adhemar said with a smile after supper.

"I do have a surprise for you, Peredis," said Robert mysteriously.

"A surprise for me?"

"Come." Robert led them outside and across the yard to the stables.

Peredis had to adjust his eyes to the gloom in the stable block before he could see what was there. It took a moment, and then he was puzzled. He was used to seeing his pony, Lightning in the nearby stall, but he wasn't there.

"Where ...?" The question was already on his lips when Robert pointed down the block to their right. Then Peredis' jaw must have dropped in amazement because both Robert and Adhemar, watching, began to laugh.

"Is that …. Is he…?"

"He's yours," Robert said. "Come and say hello to him. Then walk him around the yard. I left the bridle on for you."

Peredis went up to the further stall and stared in wonder at the beautiful black horse agitating his head as he approached. "Does he have a name?"

"Yes, his name is Ximista, which means 'lightning' in the local tongue, so it's almost the same name as your pony."

"Ximista, Ximista. He's beautiful," the young man whispered, and his hand travelled up to the horse's ears and across the forehead, feeling the silkiness of his coat and tracing the star-like flash of white that gave him his name.

"Let's give him a walk around." Robert and Adhemar stood out of the way as Peredis took the bridle and led him outside.

Robert looked on with satisfaction as they walked around the yard while Peredis talked quietly, getting the horse used to his voice.

"He's been well trained," Robert said. "And he's biddable, no funny tricks. He should be just right for you."

"Oh, I think so," he could hardly speak for happiness. "I can't believe he's mine."

"You have some time to get to know him better before you return to Eremore," Robert said encouragingly. "Enjoy him just for the moment in the yard, and we'll take him out tomorrow."

"Thank you so much."

He was still without words to thank his uncle but already at the height of his excitement he was quietly forming a bold plan, and it would include his new companion, his beautiful Ximista.

The next day, Peredis rode out on Ximista with Robert beside him for extra safety. They took the river path leading into the higher valleys, then the long circuit of the forest. After that Peredis insisted he would go alone in spite of Robert's caution. He wanted to let off steam and roared off at speed, urging Ximista forward. When he got back it was plain he'd been pushing the horse more than he should, to Robert's dismay. Robert made him sponge the mount down and kept him stabled for two days, walking the yard but no further. Peredis showed how annoyed he was, but Robert was firm.

"I know you're angry with me," Robert said, "but you have to learn discipline with a horse like Ximista." Peredis stormed off to his room and didn't speak for the rest of the day. He felt bad but really didn't know why.

"Something is troubling him still," Adhemar said to Robert. "It's unlike him to behave like this."

Still in a foul mood, Peredis went down to the village after supper. David, a boyhood friend, lived there and they had spent many an hour playing together when younger. He found David and his father busy lambing in their barn.

"I want to show you my new horse," Peredis said.

"We're a bit busy right now," his friend called out. "Some other time, Peredis."

Peredis frowned as he trudged back to La Motte, at odds with everyone and everything. He felt terrible, and as if he didn't belong anywhere. It was evening now and he had a mad idea. He would walk up to the woods and see if he could trap a young boar where they came down at dusk to dig around in the meadows. He took a staff and a net from the outhouse and set off up the hill. No doubt it was a foolish thing to do, but he had an urge to feel excitement. With a sensation of shock he suddenly had an image of the tapestry at Eremore before him. It was a vivid picture of life and death, and that was just what he needed to give himself a thrill. His father's blood was rising in him, straight from the battlefield of his ancestors.

He was so absorbed with that image that he didn't see the mother boar emerge from the trees above him and raise her snout as she picked up his scent. A moment later she was charging with her tusk aimed directly at him, screaming with fury as she went to protect the young close behind. Peredis turned to run and slipped on the wet grass of the field, barely making it to his feet. Scrambling, he managed to reach a fence surrounding a water butt into which the boar's tusk crashed as he took refuge. Confused, the animal turned away to retrieve her young and lead them to another area of the meadow.

Breathing heavily, Peredis dropped the staff and the net and fled down the hillside towards the house. He burst through the kitchen back door, alarming the housekeeper and Robert who were discussing meals.

"What on earth?" Robert exclaimed, seeing his muddy clothes and breathless state. "Are you alright?"

It took a while to get the whole story out of him, reluctant as he was to tell Robert how foolish he'd been.

"You do know, or should know by now," Robert said, "that the boar is extremely dangerous when it has young to look after."

"I didn't think ..." Peredis stammered. "I thought the little ones would be easy to catch."

"Far from it," Robert said. "With the mother beside them, you were lucky to get away without injury. That tusk can kill."

# Chapter 5

After his unfortunate mistake with the boar, Peredis spent many hours reflecting on the happier days of his childhood. There had been peaceful and prosperous days in Heimhaven where his father was not only respected and honoured, but loved, too. With their exuberant welcome, the crowds often left Doromea in no doubt of that.

As his mother herself told him later, arriving at such a dark and bare volcanic landscape she had felt she was living in a dream. This new world across the ocean could not be more different from the fertile wooded lands of old Eremore. Along Heimhaven's rocky coast, menacing plumes of steam rose from fissures in the black earth, and she had truly wondered what she had come to. She had followed her man to a land of ice and fire.

"What do you think?" Aenvar asked her as they sailed past the vast glaciers of the southern coast and the inlet approach to Heimhaven came ever closer. She nodded breathlessly.

"It's ... beautiful," she said.

"It is beautiful," he responded. "Not what you're used to, though," he smiled. "When my ancestors arrived here they thought they'd come to the land of the devil and the gates of hell awaited them."

"Are you trying to scare me?" she laughed.

"Not one bit," came his jocular reply.

She looked across the dark sea to that forbidding shore. In her mind's eye, she saw the trials and hardship ahead, but she had chosen her path and would take it, however difficult, to the very end. With great pain in her heart, mingled with great hope, she had left Eremore to be with Aenvar. Love had demanded its sacrifice and there was no return. She had paid the price and now there was only the thought of being beside him, in life and death.

At the head of the ramp where they disembarked, a stocky man in a black leather jacket waited to greet them. The two men shook hands and embraced briefly.

"Doromea," said Aenvar, turning to introduce her. "My cousin, Ari. He's been standing in for me while I was away."

"We have a welcome planned for the evening," Ari said, with a curt nod to Doromea. "You have time to rest first."

He cleared a path for them through the noisy pressing crowd and led them to a carriage where a driver waited.

"You'll want the official carriage back, I guess," said Ari with a curious smile. "I rather got to like being chauffeured around. The driver will pick you up at eight. Till this evening, then."

They swept through the crowd, waving from the back seat of the carriage as if they were royalty and so made their way through the thronged streets to the edge of town. Alone at last in the privacy of the Chieftain's residence, they could still hear the cries of welcome outside and, arm in arm, they crossed to an open window to acknowledge the warmth and enthusiasm of the people filling the square.

"They certainly do love you," said Doromea with a contented smile, waving back to the crowds.

"They would follow me anywhere," said Aenvar.

"I hope it won't come to that," she replied firmly, putting a gentle hand on his arm. She shivered suddenly as the chill of the northern air blew over the land.

# Chapter 6

They celebrated their marriage soon afterwards on the ceremonial field of Heimhaven, and Peredis was born, a chieftain's son, within the year. So his very first memories were of Hvideland, the white land, a land of snow and ice. As soon as he could walk, he accompanied his father everywhere, even on his tours of official business around the townships and farms of the island. He loved to have his son alongside him on these trips because he knew that one day, as hereditary chieftain, Peredis would walk in his shoes. Like Aenvar and his ancestors, Peredis would come to hold the fourfold axe, the mystical emblem of a chieftain's power.

As a young child he had no inkling of this, of course, only that in some way their lives were privileged and special. Not all was formality, though. On his father's days off, they went fishing in the Sound or trekking on skis around the trails laid down in the frozen landscape. Days like this ended in the hot springs where they bathed or swam all the year round, whatever the outside temperature.

Those years were good for all. It was wonderful for Peredis, too, to see how much his parents loved each other. Aenvar adored his Doromea, admired her, and would do anything for her. He even had a portrait painted of her which took pride of place in the residence. Peredis always loved that portrait. It captured her beauty and her happiness in a magical smile that lit up her face. She wore a band of pearls holding back her hair. A silver locket hung around her neck, engraved with the letter D, the same as the little silver box which she had given him and which his father carried on him always.

Life was very different when his father went away, which he did for weeks at a time as the crisis in Europa unfolded. Safe at home in Heimhaven, far from the wars of course, the boy Peredis knew nothing of these developments. He grew up with the stories of the Winter Isles exciting his imagination. His nurse Birna was a great storyteller and she loved to scare him, though his mother did not always approve. Northern tales can be harsh and cruel, full of bloodshed, decapitations, spells, ghosts, imps, mischief and sorcery. They tell of evil spirits sent to kill or do harm to others. They also tell of the "hidden folk" who dwell in mounds and rocks and don't like to be disturbed. These elves are creatures of the early creation but have not evolved and remain primitive beings, far distant in the order of things from the realm of humans or the ethereal domain of Eremore.

Yes, he sensed that early on. Most Hvidelanders were faithful to his father. As he himself had said, they would follow him anywhere. But others were less loyal. The ways of politics and power surrounded them, and where you have power, you find envy. Neither Peredis nor his mother liked it when his father went away, mainly because of the sinister presence of his cousin Ari who took charge in his absence. Ari was a man the young Peredis never liked, from his earliest contact with him. He didn't like the way he looked at him, as if he wished he wasn't there. Nor did he treat his mother with the respect that was due. Peredis knew she didn't trust him, and she had an intuition about people that rarely failed her. She spoke to Aenvar about her suspicions, but there was little she could bring in evidence other than her own deep-seated misgiving. She sensed more than him that there was some resentment in the land towards his mixed race marriage. Blinded with love, Aenvar couldn't see it. But Ari saw it all too well and, as it turned out later, was using that disquiet in plotting for his own ends.

Peredis was about six years old when he began to hear that events across the ocean were becoming critical. His father let his anxiety show in conversations with his most trusted followers. The European parliament had been dissolved and a new and powerful federation, Europus, was set up to bind the nations into a single mega-state. Appeals for help were arriving daily as an era of repression took over. Every ally, large or small, prepared to join the flag of freedom. Even Eremore promised to send forces to join the resistance that his father led. The cause was now in dire need and facing an implacable enemy, the newly formed Rational and Scientific Party, along with its extremist allies.

As Peredis heard his father say to a close friend, it was a call to arms. He could no longer ignore the cries for help, and the day soon came for his departure. He had often gone away to support the cause of the so-called Visionaries, but this time it was different. For the first time ever Peredis felt his mother was afraid. She warned him not to go.

As the militia mustered on the square before the Chieftain's residence, she kept out of sight. She didn't want the people to see the sadness written on her face. And Peredis, of course, close by her, couldn't understand. He wanted to cheer with the crowds and give the men a great send-off but somehow he realised this time he couldn't leave his mother's side. And so from an inner room of the house, they stood together and listened to the men gathering. They heard the rallying beat of the drum. They heard the tread of men marching down to the port with Aenvar at the head of the column. As he strode off holding the Chieftain's axe aloft, he must have looked up to the window, hoping to see his family for one last moment. Then he was gone. They had made their goodbyes earlier in private, and now destiny called. It was 2122, the year that the new masters of Europus called 'The Turning Point'. Nothing would ever be the same again.

\*\*\*

The time that followed was hard, especially for Peredis' mother. News came piecemeal from the old continent, none of it encouraging. In the City, friends and allies of the Visionaries were pursued, rounded up and imprisoned. Aenvar's militia had some success in skirmishes but could only really wage a guerilla warfare against the overpowering strength of the federalists. Slowly but surely the resistance was contained in a narrow coastal area of the south, and had to retreat to a fortified position on the edge of the mountains, called the Peak of Larroun. It was said that the federal army was gathering for a final assault on the rebels' last stronghold, then there came a terrible silence as everyone waited to hear the worst.

Peredis never forgot the day they brought home his father's body. A sea fog hung over the inlet and the harbour, dense and grey. The same folk who had once come down to cheer Aenvar's arrival with Doromea now stood in grim silence, waiting for the appearance of the boat that carried him. The very seabirds were still, silently gathered on cables and posts.

Peredis and his mother stood near the ramp where they would disembark. She had covered her head with a black veil to hide her tears. The boy remembered holding her hand and feeling how cold it was.

A distant slow drumbeat was heard from far off, coming closer and closer. Peredis stared into the mist, trying to catch the first glimpse of the boat. Then it glided into view, a black-painted ketch with the draped coffin on the deck. Men stood by to throw the warps and the boat tied up at the quayside. Four men from the vessel lifted the coffin and bore it slowly down the ramp, stopping in front of Doromea and her son. She put a hand on the coffin and lowered her head as if praying. Then she took the boy's hand and placed it beside hers. They stayed like that, still and quiet, for a few moments, then she stood back and let the men proceed on their way. Peredis and his mother followed behind, to the slow beat of the drum which went before them.

In solemn procession, the body was taken to the entrance hall of the residence so the people could come and pay their respects all that day and that night, with the burial planned for the third day, as tradition demanded.

Peredis remembered there was a strange mood in the air, something important but unspoken. When these things happen, you can tell there's a tension unresolved. On one hand people show their respect for the past. On the other they're already taking positions for the future. Even as a child, he could see that. He watched the groups gather, he saw the whispered conversations. All know how the phrase goes: The King is dead, long live the King. A new Chieftain would succeed as Peredis was still only a child, and would hold the power until he was eighteen. But there was a problem. The fourfold axe, emblem of the Chieftain's authority, had been lost on the battlefield and disappeared in the fray. For the Hvelanders this was a tragedy, as the axe had been handed down from Chieftain to Chieftain for centuries. It was reputed to have powers which only the rightful chieftain could inherit. Listening to all that went on, it became apparent that Ari was already presenting himself as the rightful heir. And there were others who, for their own reasons, backed his claim.

Amongst these manoeuvres, three of the men who had carried the coffin came to see Peredis' mother and asked to speak privately. Two looked like well travelled sailors, with that gait that men of the sea come to have. The other man was equally weather-beaten but taller, distinguished, with the air of a gentleman farmer.

While all this happened, Peredis wandered the residence feeling lost and confused, not knowing where he fitted in these events. Downstairs and across the square hundreds still queued to walk past his father's coffin, draped with the national flag. Others continued to gather in corners with hushed conversations and every time they saw Ari he was engaged with one group or another, gesticulating, persuading.

In a side room, in private, Doromea was having talks with the three men who, as was found out later, were carrying messages sent by Aenvar himself. Before long she summoned Peredis into the room to join them. As he went in, he saw Ari turn and watch with suspicion in his eyes. He must have been wondering what was taking place behind closed doors.

On the other side of those doors, his mother took him by the hand and led him to the three men waiting there.

"I want you to meet these friends and allies of your father," she said, "who have come to help us in our time of need. Nestor and Gorka," she indicated the two men of the sea, "brought your father back home in spite of great danger to themselves." Peredis studied the two of them carefully as they could not have been more different. The one called Nestor was short and stocky, dressed in a kind of sea-going blue overall which he never saw him change from that time on. His companion, to Peredis' surprise, was a muscular dark-skinned man with vivid blue eyes. Peredis was captivated by his appearance and must have made it all too obvious, as he stared at Peredis in a way which made him lower his gaze. Indeed, Gorka was probably as curious about him at that meeting as Peredis was himself. Little did Peredis know the sea farer was to become his best and strongest ally in so much that lay ahead.

"This gentleman," his mother said, turning towards the third man, "is Robert Montvallier, a friend of your father's."

Robert smiled, held out a hand and gave Peredis a courteous bow, saying, "Young man, I hope we will be friends, too."

Peredis took an immediate liking to him as he took his hand. He had a kind face, with wrinkles that came from smiling and good humour, not from anger or tension. The boy felt safe with him, especially after all the emotion and uncertainty of recent days.

"Your father was a wonderful man," Robert said as he brought his other hand over and Peredis' small hand was completely enclosed. It felt comfortable and safe. Peredis breathed deeply. Here was someone solid and reliable, he told himself.

He still had no idea what had been discussed between them in that room, but he sensed that something secret and momentous was about to happen. As far as the world outside was concerned, the formalities carried on as normal for the three days of mourning, up to the burial of his father in the national cemetery.

That was one of the saddest, and coldest, days of his life. He felt his legs and feet freezing as he stood in the cemetery listening to the laments and the memorial speeches. At last it was over, and he was free to move again. He wandered around the town for a bit, trying to get the circulation moving in his limbs, then he went down to the port. Nestor and Gorka, the sailors, were busy on deck. He stood and watched them for a while and this time noticed the name of the boat on the prow. It was called *Kresala*.

"Are you getting ready to leave?" he called out. Nestor, the skipper, looked his way and replied, "On the night tide, lad."

"Is Robert going with you?" Peredis asked, rather dreading the answer.

Nestor and Gorka looked at each other a moment before the skipper spoke again.

"You should ask your mother that question," he said. "In fact," he went on, "you should really be up at the residence, you know. She may be needing you ..."

His voice tailed away. Then came Gorka's resonant tone, strong and deep, with an unfamiliar accent. "We'd best keep on, or we'll never be ready. Get along now to your mother, young man."

It was true, it seemed. His mother did need him for things, because the moment he appeared at the residence she called him upstairs and took him into her bedroom. Peredis was taken aback to find her packing suitcases.

"What's this?" He caught his breath. "Are you leaving me too?" A cold tremor went through him and he must have looked in total shock, as she came to him quickly and embraced him.

"Come and sit on the bed," she said, "I need to tell you why Robert is here."

"I do hope he isn't leaving," Peredis struggled to speak.

"Listen, Peredis," she held her son close to her. "Robert and you and I are all leaving tonight. That's the reason Robert is here, to take us back with him to Europa."

"I don't understand," he said. "Why?"

"It's what your father wanted. He decided he couldn't trust Ari to take care of us if anything happened to him. So he asked Robert to take us with him to La Motte, in the mountains."

"I don't like Ari," Peredis said with the simplicity of a child. "I like Robert."

"Robert promised your father he'd look after us. So we leave tonight on Nestor's boat. You must get ready the things you want to take, in a couple of bags, that's all. The men will help us down to the boat after twelve midnight. Go now and pack before we have supper."

As he started out of the room, he paused a moment. "Did you know the boat is called *Kresala*?" He said.

"No, I didn't," replied his mother, busy again with her packing.

"I wonder what it means, *Kresala*. That isn't a northern name, is it?"

"You must ask Nestor or Gorka, they'll tell you if it means anything," his mother said. "Run along now and rest on your bed until I come to wake you."

He was only half awake when she came to rouse him and led him downstairs to join Robert and Gorka waiting for them.

"We must go quietly," she said in a low voice, and they set off towards the harbour, moving silently in the shadows. Holding tightly on to his mother's hand, the boy sensed the tension and the danger without really understanding what was happening. Walking quickly, they reached the harbour, bright with lights, where a sea mist came rolling in and shrouded everything in an orange glow. Crossing the wharfs, they started down the ramp to *Kresala's* mooring. In that moment, shouts and the sound of running feet echoed from the town.

"Quick, on board!" urged Nestor from the cockpit, starting up the yacht's engine. Robert helped Peredis and his mother on to the deck as Gorka ran to slip the mooring line at the prow. Then the *Kresala* turned seawards as Nestor cast off astern, gave the engine throttle and glided into the mist, leaving the shore behind. The shouts and cries from the dockside sounded louder and more shrill as a band of men reached the ramp and stood there powerless to stop them. Peredis and his mother looked back through the swirling mist and he was sure he could see Ari among them, gesticulating angrily. They had only just made it in time.

What does *Kresala* mean? Peredis remembered asking Nestor that very question as they motored through the mist and out of Heimhaven harbour.

"In my tongue it means the salt spray of the sea," Nestor said, his eyes fastened on the channel leading to the Sound. Peredis noticed as their ocean journey continued that his eyes changed colour like the sea itself, sometimes slate grey, sometimes aquamarine, sometimes green.

"And what is your tongue?"

"Vasconian," he said, then leaving no time to ask more questions, "Get those fenders on board for me, lad. You might as well work for your passage."

The boy ran to do his bidding. What a thrill it was to feel he belonged, to be one of the crew of that fine yacht heading out across the waters where he and his father had often fished, and so onward to the mighty ocean itself.

As they hit the choppy waters of the Sound, he was breathless with excitement, feeling the spray hit his face. It was as if the pain and uncertainty of all they had passed through, he and his mother, was being washed away by that very same salt.

# Chapter 7

At the end of their journey across the ocean, Robert's home of La Motte awaited them in its peaceful valley. But Peredis couldn't say his first months in the mountains brought him peace. He found himself longing to be back on the high seas and even lay awake at night planning to run away to sea, every youngster's dream.

It was another thing altogether for the boy to live through his mother's decline. They say a heart once broken cannot be healed. With Aenvar's death, Peredis' mother had lost everything. She had renounced her people and gone into exile. She had embraced mortality. Now it must have seemed to her that nothing was left. There is no cure for devastating loss. Her son watched her slip away slowly, worn down by grief. It was like an illness that invaded her, drawing her into its dark depths from which there was no return. He wanted, needed, to cling all the closer to her. Something in him was dying with her.

She knew that, for my sake, one vital journey remained before she could give way. She had to free him from the choices she'd made, and the only place that could be achieved was in Eremore itself. The law required that any child of her union with Aenvar, in order to receive their rights and duties, had to be presented to the court of Eremore. So my mother took me as a child and passed through the mountain gateway for one last journey in her lifetime to fulfil what was required. Her father the king, Odolf at the time, greeted her sorrowfully and presided over the private ceremony. He himself became Peredis' Eremorean father and gave him a silver dagger as a token. The event was recorded in the Annals, but never published openly. He remembered the magical journey they made through the heart of the mountains, the thrill of the boat slipping down the underground river through caverns sparkling with crystals, then the amazing sight of that overarching copper sky that shelters Eremore from dangers and the Outside.

After that, nothing is clear. Only years later did he come to accept Eremore as a part of his very being.

After their return to La Motte, her duty now fulfilled, his mother withdrew more and more to her room and lay in semi-darkness with the shutters closed. Towards the autumn of that first year, the inevitable end finally came. The effort to live became too hard for her. She barely communicated, even with her son. But one day, she called him to her and dried the tears running down his cheeks.

"Peredis," she whispered. "Take this." She showed him the little silver box in her hand. "Take it," she urged. Peredis clutched it in his palm and gazed at her, trying to grasp what she wanted.

"One day," she went on as her eyes flickered and her voice faded, "this token will bring you your dream. And my salvation, too, for the one who holds this token will redeem me from my fate."

"What do you mean?" He asked with anguish, desperate to do her will but feeling only lost and confused.

"I mean everything will turn out well," she smiled, stroking his cheek. "You must never be afraid. Believe and you'll find happiness. All will be well."

"All will be well," he repeated. "All will be well."

She held his hand and he knew from her touch that strength was failing her.

"I have to go on a journey," she whispered as her breathing became shallow. "Your father's waiting for me."

"Don't leave me," the boy said hoarsely, hardly able to speak.

"Robert will look after you. He's a good man."

"I know," he said, pressing her hand to his face. "But ..." Then he stopped. "Yes, he's a good friend to me." In his innocent way, he was trying to reassure her, perhaps even give her permission to go.

"I've put protection around you both," she murmured, and he strained to hear her words now. "You're safe here. La Motte will be your home."

After those words, silence. They hadn't noticed but Robert had entered the room and was standing behind him, his hands on Peredis' shoulders. He said nothing, and they stayed there, like that, for a long while as we watched his mother go down into her last sleep.

As we left the room to go downstairs, Robert stopped on the landing and turned to the portrait which he had brought from Heimhaven at Doromea's request.

"Do you see the mystery?" he said in a quiet voice.

Peredis looked up and saw straight away the change in the painting. The beauty of that smile which had enraptured his father and which he had wanted to capture in the image had gone from her face. Sadness was now written in her eyes as she gazed outwards towards some unresolved desire. Secretly Peredis clutched the little silver box, held firmly in his hand. It was and always would be the mirror of the locket around her neck. It linked him to her forever, as she had said, bringing her to salvation and Peredis to his dream.

"I do believe," he told himself as he lay sleepless at night, grieving and knowing only sorrow.

At that time he had no other faith but his belief in those words and no way of knowing the future, and no way of seeing through the darkness. He was still only eight years old.

# Chapter 8

His life was about to change again. He remembered the day well as he'd spent the afternoon under the late winter sun helping Alphonse the estate worker to prune the vines and gather up the cuttings from the ground. He called them *sarments* and told Peredis they'd be used later to fire up the bread oven. It was hot and tiring work and the water bottle was empty. Peredis walked down the slope to the house to fill it with water from the kitchen tap. As he ran the water, he heard Robert speaking to someone in the entrance hall of the house and went to see who it was. Robert was embracing a tall stranger who had just arrived. He beckoned me over.

"Peredis, I want you to meet someone."

The boy walked over to greet the newcomer and looked up at him with childish fascination. He was taller and slimmer than Robert, dressed in a leather riding habit from his journey, with a pointed beard and eyes that saw straight through you. He put out a hand, and Peredis took it in his own, feeling comfortable the moment they touched. He didn't let go straight away and just looked without speaking.

"This is Adhemar de la Brèche," Robert said. "He's going to be your tutor."

"I'm very pleased to meet you, sir," the boy said. "Can you tell me what that is? A tutor? I've never had one of those before."

The stranger laughed gently, not at Peredis but with him, and the ice was broken.

He said, smiling, "And I've never been a tutor before. So I've no idea either what it is. Shall we try and find out together?"

"Yes," Peredis said firmly. "I'd like that."

Robert picked up the bags that had arrived with the stranger, saying, "Adhemar will be staying in the tower. He knows the way." The tower was a square defence situated in the corner of the walled property, at the far end of the gardens. It had a small sitting room on the ground level from which a stone staircase led up to a bedroom and another room on the upper storeys. Peredis sometimes used it as a hideout, escaping there with Robert's dogs Orlando and Oliver, when he wanted to be on his own and wrestle with his thoughts. The two pointers were always good company for him.

Now the tower was to have a special place in his life. For seven years, it was to become a fountain of learning and discovery. He was only allowed in the downstairs room, though, which Adhemar lined with books. The tutor slept upstairs and a further upper room was his private domain. Up there, he was not to be disturbed in his researches, chemical, biological, anatomical, who knows ... That side of him was a complete mystery.

It was decided Peredis would go to Adhemar every morning at eight o'clock for our sessions, whatever they were to be. The boy was filled with curiosity as he had no idea at all what we were supposed to be doing together. The very first day, the very first session, was something of an eye-opener.

Peredis arrived punctually at eight and entered

the little sitting room where Adhemar was reading in an armchair with a long pipe in his hand from which he breathed out occasional sweet smelling clouds of smoke. A green tobacco pouch lay on the table at his side.

"Ah," he cried, looking up. "We can begin."

"Begin what?" Peredis asked as respectfully as he could.

"You'll see," he got up as he spoke, "and I suppose I'll see, as well. Let's go."

Peredis followed him out of the tower, across the gardens, through the arched entrance and along a track which led to the woods. He went ahead at quite a pace leaving Peredis slightly breathless, and even more curious than before. Where was he taking him?

They arrived where the mountain stream came tumbling over rocks and pools on its way down to the river at the valley bottom. He scrambled around on the rocky edges of the stream, climbing the slope as he went, and then eventually found a place to sit comfortably with room for the two of them side by side.

"This will do nicely," he said, sitting himself down and patting the stone at his side to encourage the boy to join him.

They sat there in silence. Peredis looked at the noisy waters rushing down and after a while began to wonder if there were any trout in the pool nearby where he often went to fish. He decided that nearer the valley bottom there were broad pools. Here the water was too restless.

"No fish here," the boy declared. Adhemar made no reply, and they continued to sit silently as the stream coursed past us in endless swirls and rivulets. In places logs had got stuck between stones and caused the water to dam up, capturing loose vegetation and twigs. From time to time you could see a leafy branch come tumbling down a chute and travel across pools, only to career on downwards. In places the rocks were smooth as if polished by the waters and he thought one of them would make a good slide for plunging into the larger pool below.

Many minutes passed with many impatient ponderings as Peredis asked himself what exactly they were doing. Adhemar sat in total silence. Then the boy's perch on the rock started to feel none too comfortable and Peredis wanted to move. He went down closer to the water's edge and started throwing twigs into the torrent to see where they went. One twig caught his attention. It had a broad leaf attached to it like a sail and he decided to launch it like a boat. However his little craft didn't last long in all that turmoil and sank rapidly. He abandoned that game and squatted down with his fingers in the pool.

"Can I bathe my feet?" the boy asked.

"It'll be cold," Adhemar said. "This is snowmelt coming down from the peaks."

"I don't mind," Peredis said, taking off his shoes and socks and dipping his toes in the flow. But the cold was so intense it was unbearable. He quickly put his socks and shoes back on, rubbing his feet as he did so to bring back a little warmth.

"What do you think?" Adhemar said.

"About what?"

"About this water," he continued.

"You were right, it's freezing cold," Peredis said, scrambling back up to join him on the wide rock.

"There was once a man," Adhemar said, "who spent hours and hours just looking at water and trying to understand it."

"What is there to understand?" he asked. "It's just water, isn't it?"

"Suppose it could speak to you," his tutor said.

Peredis laughed. "That's funny."

"Funny strange or funny absurd?"

"A bit of both," the boy replied.

"This man said that in the end water spoke to him."

"Is that true? Water can speak? I don't think so."

"He certainly knew a lot about water, things which would make life better for all of us. But a good deal of what he learned died with him."

"He should have written it down."

"He tried to, but what he wrote wasn't always very clear. And anyway, the interesting part is that much of what he knew couldn't be put into words." He turned to Peredis and asked, "Do you think you could tell me in words what we've been looking at for the last thirty minutes?"

Peredis stumbled over his words as he tried to reply. "Well, I suppose ... I could just say it's a stream coming down a mountain. And the water's very cold."

"Yes," Adhemar said, "that's a good start. Let's come back tomorrow and see if we can add a little more to that. We're finished for today."

So this is what they did every day for a week, whatever the weather. Rain or shine, it didn't seem to matter to Adhemar. Caught in a downpour, they simply carried on watching the millions of raindrops pitting the stream, adding their bullet-like chaos to the torrent. By the end of that week, Peredis had got over his impatience and started to look at water as he never had before. With every half hour spent watching the stream in the same place every day, the sheer variety and complexity of the tumbling water became more and more obvious to him, its light, its shade, its movement, depth, colours, its gathering and separating, its infinite changes all coursing within the same channel.

But strangely, at the same time as Peredis saw more and more in the waters, he was left more and more at a loss for words to describe it. And then, to his surprise, something happened on the seventh day. As they sat on the broad stone and watched the rushing waters and the flying spray, Peredis had a sudden insight.

"It's all one!" he cried.

Adhemar looked at him intensely. "What did you say?"

"It's all one," Peredis repeated with a surge of enthusiasm. "I was sitting here looking at the stream but my mind went back to the ocean journey from Heimhaven. And I realised. It's all one. All the waters all over the earth are the same water, all joined up. This water is going to be the river and then the ocean, and the ocean is going to be the rain and the snow, and the rain is going to be the stream. It's the same water, everywhere. So water is all one."

Adhemar nodded quietly. He looked at his pupil again and there was a smile in his eyes.

"The water spoke to you," he said. "I wonder what else it has to tell you."

That first lesson with Adhemar, if it can be called lesson, was the first step in a journey of discovery which lasted, not days, but years. An eight year old couldn't possibly grasp the full significance of that simple insight beside a mountain stream, but it led him on surely to a knowledge and a practice that guides his life even today. Water was his first, and last, teacher.

So they went on together, Adhemar and Peredis, to discover what it meant for him to be the tutor. He opened doors, but the pupil had to pass through them himself. As Peredis was to find out, in more senses than one, Adhemar was the gate-watcher.

\*\*\*

The incident with the boar had taught Peredis a lesson, and as time went on, he settled once again into the rural life of La Motte. He became calmer and less agitated, and after he promised to treat Ximista with more care, Robert allowed him to ride out on his own.

Both Adhemar and Robert tried to have conversations with him in moments of quiet. The wound he had suffered from the tapestry continued to puzzle them but they were afraid to open the hurt before it was properly healed.

"When will I go back to Eremore?" he continued to ask. He missed the company of his fellow-students, especially his friend Anton. Then one day, out of the blue, he asked, "When can I go and see where my father died, on the battlefield of Larroun?"

Robert and Adhemar looked at each other with surprise. The question was completely unexpected.

"We don't think that would be wise as yet," Adhemar said carefully.

"Why not?"

"It's still a place of danger," said his tutor mysteriously. "And there are many traces and leftovers of battle."

"And what about my father's axe? The Chieftain's axe was left on the Peak of Larroun, we know that. It needs to be claimed," Peredis said urgently. "What happened to it after the battle?"

"We don't know," Adhemar said. "It disappeared from the battlefield and was lost, or perhaps stolen."

"The axe is yours by right," Robert confirmed, "but we think it was taken by Ari, Aenvar's cousin, but we have no proof."

"Then I must find it," Peredis cried excitedly. "If it's mine by right, I have to make that my mission. Will you help me?"

"We'll help you all we can, Peredis," said Adhemar, "but it won't be easy. There may be many obstacles on your path and we don't know where they will lead. When you are well we will go back to Eremore and ask King Odolf for his advice."

# Chapter 9

Once they had returned to Eremore, Peredis was happy to be joined again with Anton, his loyal friend, and he really enjoyed the schooling in the citadel. He got on well with his fellow students and now he was feeling fit and strong again, he threw himself with renewed energy into the life of the school. There was only one other student who bugged him for some reason, a tall thin boy called Jante, who went out of his way to annoy him, especially in the self-defence class.

"You should take no notice," said Anton. "He's just envious because of your relationship with the king. And watch how he tries to please Stephane, the Chancellor's son. Everyone knows he was rejected by your mother Doromea."

Peredis was taken aback to be reminded of this event which he had uncovered in the so-called Pages of Shame hidden away in the Red Annals.

"So that's why he's so standoffish with me."

"Of course. But it's all water under the bridge. Just steer clear of him. And Stephane, too, I guess."

But it wasn't water under the bridge for Jante, it seemed. And one day as the martial arts class came to an end he made some stupid comment about Peredis' mother. Peredis' blood rose and he leaped across the classroom and delivered a kick to Jante's chest. The boy flew backwards and landed on the floor. Then a combat began in earnest, with kicks and punches on both sides. It came to an end when Sigmund, the master, appeared in the doorway and stopped them.

"I'll speak to you in my office," he said to Peredis sternly. "Jante, leave us."

Once they were alone together, Sigmund said, "I know you were provoked but I can't have you fighting like that. If you want to fight, come to see me at the end of each day's class and I'll show you how to do it properly."

Peredis was thrilled to know that the master and himself could have sessions together. Learning one to one, they went on to make rapid progress and he was delighted when Sigmund commented on how well he was doing in only a short time. Then one day as they finished work together, Sigmund said:

"By the way, the king wants to see us. It seems he has a plan for you. So get dressed and I'll see you in the king's office in fifteen minutes."

Peredis couldn't help feeling nervous as he was ushered into the king's reception lounge. Had he done something wrong? Odolf gestured for him to sit beside Sigmund on the visitor's sofa. A moment or two later, Adhemar appeared and joined us. All eyes were now on Peredis and he was more and more apprehensive.

"We've been discussing your future, Peredis," the king began. "As you are aware, you have the blood of two royal families, through the ancestral lines of your father and your mother. That is a powerful destiny that we treasure and must care for. It also means that you must be strong enough in yourself to fulfil that destiny. Our task is to train you to be ready. We propose therefore to enlist you in the Silver Brigade. It's an elite body of men and women, some twenty in number. Master

Sigmund is the commander of the brigade, and he's about to recruit a new intake. We want you to join. From what I hear, your friend Anton will be joining as well. What do you think? Do you need more time to decide?"

Peredis felt a surge of confidence. With Anton at his side he knew he could face all sorts of obstacles. And one important thought occurred to him. Joining the Silver Brigade would surely give him much more freedom than staying in the citadel where he hadn't been able to find any records leading directly to his father's axe? He held on to that single thought.

"Well, silence is approval," said the king with a gentle smile. Adhemar nodded his agreement as well. Sigmund then gave his approval.

"We leave the citadel tomorrow morning at first light. Be ready at the city gates. We travel along the coast to our training area at Gannet's Nest. We will set up there and spend the next month on manoeuvres."

The first thing Peredis wanted was to find Anton and tell him the news. His life was about to change again. A new challenge lay ahead and he had a vision of something different and wonderful about to happen. He bade farewell to Adhemar before going to look for his friend.

"I think it's a good decision," Adhemar reassured him.

"Please tell Robert, I'm really happy about this," Peredis said. "And I promise I won't do anything stupid ...." he grinned foolishly.

"I know," Adhemar said with a knowing smile. "Those days are over."

The recruits were ready and waiting at the city gates the next morning. As they waited, they suddenly saw a figure approaching that gave no comfort at all. Peredis nudged Anton.

"Look who's coming," he said dolefully as Jante appeared in the gateway.

"Take no notice," Anton said in his usual relaxed way. "Pretend he's not there."

"I'll try to ignore him, but it's hard. He just causes me bother, he does it on purpose, too."

"I can see we're going to have fun," said Anton with a wry smile.

"Please don't say that," murmured Peredis. "He makes me feel ill."

"Anyway, we're off now. It's half an hour down the coast to Gannet's Nest, the training base. It's a lovely drive along the cliffs, so enjoy it ..."

# PART II
## Training

# Chapter 10

The vehicle stopped on the parade ground which overlooked the base. It was a beautiful spot, with views to the far horizon. Sigmund lined everyone up and got them to stand to attention. There were nine in the group, including three girls.

A tall thin man in military gear came out to join everyone and took up a position beside Sigmund.

"That's Stephane," Anton whispered to Peredis.

"Welcome to Gannet's Nest," Sigmund announced. "Your lives are about to change. You're going to be tested beyond all endurance. Before a week is past, all of you will be longing to abandon this place for the comfort and security of your homes. Half of you will give up and walk away," he said. "I can promise you that. I also promise you that if you stay the full course, if you rise to the challenge and come through the training, you will be stronger, fitter, and more aware of your own ability than you've ever been. You'll also learn to trust your fellows with your very life."

He paused and looked his recruits up and down. "You can of course leave right now if you choose. Raise your hand, step out, and by nightfall you'll be back in the citadel." He paused again while no one moved. "Nobody? Right, the programme starts tomorrow at dawn. This afternoon we want to interview each of you in the staff block which is the grey building behind me. You're billeted in the wooden bunkhouse over there. Settle yourselves in. Take your gear from the transport, find the bed space and locker allocated to you and get organised. I'll call you one by one for our initial interview. Stephane here, the base manager, will give you a guiding hand." He indicated towards his companion. "Remember, he's your superior officer though we don't wear any sign of rank, and he is to be obeyed instantly and without question whatever he tells you to do. Carry on."

They all collected from the transport the small amount of gear they'd been allowed to bring and trooped into their new home which turned out to be a long bare shell with rows of slatted beds with thin mattresses. Each bed had a table on one side and a tall wooden cupboard with open shelves on the other, already supplied with a set of kit for each recruit.

Peredis had only just settled in with his few possessions on the shelves, when he was the first to be summoned to the staff office. Sigmund and Stephane sat on one side of their desk. Peredis was left standing.

Sigmund spoke first. "We know you had a bout of illness which has taken you time to recover. We shall be keeping an eye on you. We also know you have issues with your fellow-student Jante. Or perhaps better put, he has issues with you. We don't want to see any conflict between you. The Silver Brigade is a brotherhood not a war zone. I'm sure Stephane agrees."

His colleague nodded in agreement. "We will be very severe towards any bad attitude or hostility. The fact is that we have deliberately put you with Jante in order to test your self-control. Don't let us or yourself down. And bear in mind that any delinquent behaviour could mean immediate dismissal from the Brigade. Do you understand?"

"Yes, sir, I understand."

"Call in Jante," said Sigmund.

While the officers carried on with their interviews, Peredis went back to the bunkhouse and got to know his fellow recruits. There were three girls, Rowena, Edurne and Itxaso, who all looked very fit and were clearly well trained. Then came half a dozen lads, very different in style: Hani, Bar, Conor and Allan, and of course, Jante and Anton. Peredis knew some of them by sight from the class at school. This was a chance to know them better now. One of them who had an honest and cultured look to him was called Conor of the Six. He came from one of the nine families of Eremore and had a distinguished background. He told Peredis it was traditional in his family to offer recruits to the Brigade.

Peredis liked the look of Hani, a rugged, muscular young man, as well as Allan and Eruvin, equally tough in appearance. A little fellow called Bar was the exception in the group, small and slight, with a constant smile and a laugh which made him popular.

Having got to know his comrades, Peredis went off to sit with Anton overlooking the ocean. "I hope Jante is getting the same lecture they gave me," he said.

"We'll wait and see," said Anton. Then, changing the subject, "They seem a nice crowd," he said.

"You mean the girls?" Peredis asked with a smile, gesturing towards the group of three who were sitting together a short distance away.

"I like the look of Rowena," said Anton. "She has the air of a serious athlete. We'll see how fit she is when we start doing proper exercises tomorrow. I've heard the initial training is pretty tough with some real mountain work towards the end. "

Peredis couldn't have been happier to hear that. His mission to search for the axe would surely take him into the hills and valleys of the south. He welcomed the news that the Silver Brigade routine would toughen him up for whatever challenge lay ahead.

# Chapter 11

Sure enough, the sounding of a bell woke them all at an early hour and within minutes they were all up and running, heading first down a path to the Five Mile Beach below Gannet's Nest, then dipping into a sea pool, followed by a cliff climb and the return run to the base. Peredis was pleased to find he could keep up with the pace, and even more pleased to see that Jante came well behind him, about fifth in the squad.

This gruelling exercise was to be their daily routine. The rest of the morning consisted of classwork, practice and familiarity with equipment.

One of the best moments of the day was the hour after lunch when lessons were done, exercises were finished and it was good to lie down for half an hour at least. Anton and himself sat out in their favourite spot on the cliff edge enjoying the sea breeze and the patterns of clouds as far as the horizon.

Peredis went as usual to lie down for the restful half hour. Then there came an almighty crash from within the bunkhouse. Anton leaped to his feet and rushed in to see what had happened. His friend's bed had somehow come adrift and he lay sprawled on the floor. He was shocked rather than hurt. Conor and Allan who had been resting in the bunkhouse at the same time came quickly to see if they could help. Allan who was of a mechanical mind started to examine the bed closely.

"A screw has been loosened," he said.

At this moment they heard a strange noise coming from Jante's direction in the background. A noise like laughter being suppressed.

"It must have been deliberate," Allan said, frowning. "It's easily mended but someone has helped it come apart. I'll get some tools from the staff office and make sure it's tight and secure." He went off, leaving Peredis seething with anger.

Peredis looked towards Jante and clenched his fists. He was about to explode with fury but Anton put out a restraining hand and turned him away. "Stay calm, Peredis," he said. "He wants you to lose your cool. Allan will fix it."

He led his friend outside to breathe deeply and take the air. Conor followed. "We know who's responsible," he said. "But there's no proof. Normally we should tell Sigmund, but ..."

The three of them looked at each other in quiet understanding.

"We're with you, Peredis," said Conor, "all the way."

Peredis showed his gratitude with a quick embrace of his fellows. He realised with a surge of emotion that the brotherhood of the Brigade was like nothing he had ever experienced in his life.

# Chapter 12

Peredis didn't let Jante's nasty little schemes get the better of him. A missing shoe, a bar of soap in his pillow, a lost pen for his schoolroom notes .... he worked out in his own mind that these annoying things were sent to test him. But he was looking out for the chance to get his own back. It came one night when everyone was doing a tracking game in the forest, called 'bagging'. The squad was set loose, each of them on their own, and had to see how many of their fellows they could capture by ambushing them and putting a bag over their head. Peredis thought he should be good at the game with his hunting experience in the woods around La Motte. Anton, Conor and himself decided they would ignore the rest and concentrate on capturing Jante.

Their scheme worked to perfection. Between the three of them wearing masks they managed to ambush their enemy, bag him and then tied his hands around a tree, leaving him there to be found by the others. After that they went separately back to base and waited for the remaining hunters to appear.

"You weren't quite following the rules there, were you? Where's Jante?" Sigmund said as they waited in front of the office. Peredis grinned happily. Sigmund shook his head in mild disapproval, but couldn't resist a smile.

"You'll have to go and find him," he said. "You can't leave him out there all night."

"Of course not, master. I'll go and rescue him."

"I thought that was a good trick of yours with Jante …" Rowena said. She had come over to sit with them in the lunch break. "I don't care for him very much, and I don't like the way he tries to get close to us girls."

"Stephane says we're due for another trial next week," Edurne said. She and Itxaso had formed a friendship as they both came from the same village not that far from La Motte.

"Did he say where?" Anton asked.

"Towards the south, glacier country."

"And what will we have to do?"

"It's called orienteering. They drop us off along the coast somewhere and give us a map and a compass to find our way back."

"Sounds fun," said Conor.

"The fun bit is that we go in pairs," said Edurne. "And Peredis will have more fun than most as Stephane said he's pairing with Jante." She chuckled wickedly.

"Oh, no," Peredis groaned. "Must I?"

"They're putting you to the test again," said Anton. "It's a bit unfair, isn't it?"

"Perhaps you'll get extra points with Jante along with you," Conor said with a laugh.

"Well, thanks for that encouragement," Peredis said with a wry smile.

Half way through the second week, they were presented with their first major task off base. They would separate into four pairs and be transported to the southern mountains. Each couple was given a destination, navigating from the position where they were dropped.

At the destination they'd find a letterbox with orders for the next step, and so on. The basic aim was to beat the other teams back to the finishing point on the coast road. This was all they were told before they kitted up and boarded the transport. But first they had to go to Stephane in the office and find out who their partner was and get their climbing equipment, maps, compass and readings. Peredis was appalled to find it was confirmed. He was partnered with Jante and, even worse, Jante was the leader in charge of their pair. Whether he wanted it or not, they were going to have to work together.

"You never know, he might surprise you ...," Anton said wisely as they parted, each to his own task.

Jante and Peredis were the third pair to be dropped off, some miles south of the citadel and on the edge of rounded foothills rising to a mountain range in the distance, high peaks with snow-cover reaching up to touch Eremore's copper sky through the Shield. This was almost certainly the area of the Great Glacier which he'd heard of as a boy at La Motte. There were said to be secret passes up there between Eremore and the Outside.

Jante studied the map and found the first way-point due east. They set off and after about three hours' walking, arrived in a grassy plain where horses and cattle were grazing.

Halfway up the northern slope they came to a ruined sheep pen beside a water trough overflowing into a muddy morass. According to the instructions, this should be the site of the first letterbox and, sure enough, they saw a lidded red tin container attached to the stone gable of the building. Picking their way around the mud, they went to open it up and took out the folded paper. The message said they next had to make for the Dragon's Beak, a vertiginous cleft that cut through the mountain range to the north.

"I think we've done the easy bit," Peredis muttered to himself.

"What was that?" Jante turned challengingly towards his companion.

"I said that was the easy part so far," Peredis repeated. "The real challenge is to come."

"We're going to be first today," Jante asserted. He had an aggressive look in his eye which Peredis didn't trust.

"Come on, we're not going to let those others beat us."

Peredis said nothing, but trailed along behind as Jante set off at a vigorous pace. It wasn't long before they found the ground boggy and slow going, the trees a mass of broken and twisted pines difficult to work their way through.

For some time they continued to scale the upper reaches, wending their way over broken ground where they had to step with caution. At the top they came out on a platform overlooking a deep escarpment that fell away sharply below them. The view from there was tremendous, an endless succession of low green hills rolling away into the far distance and Peredis wanted to spend a few moments enjoying the view but Jante was impatient to move on.

"Come on," he said sharply. "No time to waste. We must find the next instructions." Jante stood up again, smiling to himself.

After a bit of a search, the next letterbox was found half buried in a cairn of stones. They took out the folded paper and Jante read the orders. All it said was, "Find your quickest way back to the finish point."

"Very helpful," Peredis commented with a bitter laugh. "What do you think, my leader?" The question was rather mocking, and it really annoyed Jante. He stared at the map in his hands and tried to make sense of it.

"Let me have a look." Taking the map from him Peredis quickly saw the problem, as well as why they'd been given it to solve. They were on a blind overhang and couldn't see what was below, only that the map showed a fall in altitude of around seven hundred feet. It was clear that the escarpment offered the quickest way down to the valley bottom which would then take them west, following a river down to the sea. But could they really descend a cliff of seven hundred feet with the equipment they had? At worst, the way down might be sheer vertical rockface.

"If we jumped, we could be there in no time," Peredis joked, but Jante didn't see the humour. He was finding it hard to decide. But then his conclusion took Peredis by surprise.

"We'll go straight down," he declared. "But first I need to look over the edge and see what's there. You'll have to secure me as I look over and then pull me back up."

He unpacked and put on his harness while Peredis wound a climbing rope around a pointed rock to hold him secure and put on gloves to control the rope. Then Jante attached himself and eased back until he was right on the lip of the precipice and able to look down.

"Haul me back," he ordered, and they both reeled in the slack until he was safely back on the platform.

"What did you see?" Peredis asked.

Jante took a moment to recover his breath. "It isn't just rock below, there's quite a bit of shrubs and trees," he said, "and it isn't all vertical. The first bit is the worst. Once you're past the overhang you could almost slide down in parts. I think we should try it."

"What if we get stuck half way down?" Peredis questioned.

"We'll face that when we get to it," Jante said in a commanding voice. "I'm in charge and that's my decision."

"Well, I hope you're right," said Peredis doubtfully. "Are you going to lead off then?"

"Yes, I'll go down the first stretch while you anchor me up here, then I'll make the rope secure and you can come down and go past me to hammer in the next peg below. And we'll carry on like that, overlapping each other."

"Let's try it," Peredis said, not entirely convinced. He kept his doubts to himself as Jante put on his harness and hammered a peg into a crack in the rock platform, then ran the rope through the ring at the end. When he was satisfied it was secure, he gave a signal to Jante to carry on. As the rope went slack he gave a shout and let himself swing beneath the overhang. A few feet below, Peredis joined him on a grassy ledge.

"There's no going back now," he said grimly. Jante nodded.

"I'll keep going down," he said, and started to descend the rope a few feet further down to where they could hammer in a new safety peg. For the next few stages they were able to slither down patches of vegetation or slide happily on loose scree where they didn't even bother to attach ropes. Riding down these scree slopes was an exhilarating run, but their luck ran out when one of these thrilling slides came to a sudden end over a vertical drop. Shouting a warning, Peredis grabbed on to the nearest branch at hand to break his fall, only to feel it come away in his hand. The next moment he fell backwards several feet and crashed into a tangled bunch of saplings which brought him to a breathless halt. He heard Jante's voice calling from some way above.

"Peredis, are you OK? Peredis! Peredis!"

He tried to call back but was completely winded after suffering a blow in the fall which sent a stabbing pain through his ribs with every breath.

"Peredis? Answer me!"

Peredis tried again to take a deep breath but it was shallow, lacking any force. From the distance came the sound of Jante's voice, shouting something.

Then he heard Jante say, "Don't move or you'll fall. I'm coming down," and his body stiffened in shock again.

There was silence for a while until Peredis could hear movement, scratching and sliding. Stones and dust were falling around him. He dared to open his eyes and saw Jante coming down with ropes leading back to the top of the cliff. Another minute and Jante was at his side, securing the harness. He jammed two nuts into cracks in the rock and clipped both of them on.

"You're safe now," he said, panting with the effort. "First tell me if you can move, and how hurt you are."

"I was winded in the fall. Got a nasty bang in the ribs, but my rucksack saved me from the worst. I'm getting my breath back now," Peredis said cautiously. "I think I'll be able to sit up in a moment or two."

"Right. Now we have to figure out how to get you out of here." Jante both looked and sounded in charge, and Peredis was happy to let him make the decisions. "Stay still for the moment," he said, "while I sort out these ropes. You've got a five hundred foot drop below you."

He unclipped a number of looped cords from his harness and deftly began to fix sliding knots to his own rope, until he'd rigged up a system for ascending. Peredis watched with admiration as he worked away silently, winding each cord around the ascending rope, then pulling it down through a clip.

"You see how this works," he said, pointing to the knots. "You put your foot in the lower loop, let it take your weight, then pull yourself up with the loop above."

"Yes," his partner was able to say with renewed breath, "we were practising this on the beach cliff last week."

"Exactly," Jante nodded and smiled. "Didn't think we'd need this so soon, did we?" For Peredis it was the first time he'd ever seen a smile from him.

"Now," he said, "put your weight in the loops, and we'll ascend one step at a time. I'll go up beside you and pull up the slack as we go."

What followed was slow and tiring but by taking it step by step they managed to rejoin the scree where Jante had anchored them both to a stout tree. Here they stopped for a pause to get their breath back.

"We need to find a way across to that wooded part of the escarpment," Jante pointed to where the trees were taller and thicker. "Those are larch woods. We can use the trees to take us down bit by bit even if it's quite steep. Do you think you can make it?"

"I'm fine," said Peredis, though he was still grimacing with pain. "Nothing's broken, I think."

Jante gathered up the ropes and coiled them, then fed one of them through a brake on his harness. "Just to be on the safe side," he explained. "I'll lead the way."

Their progress didn't get any easier. The escarpment drop seemed to go on down forever but they were committed to descending and there was no way back. Most of the time they couldn't see what dangers were below them and had to judge where the slope was likely to be safe and where impassable. Jante turned out to have a skill for this, checking the terrain below us as they went down. Somehow he avoided any sudden obstacles and guided them successfully down to the river valley below.

Looking back, for a long time Peredis could only feel gratitude for Jante's ability and their survival. As they both lay exhausted at the river's edge, he managed to voice his thanks. "You saved my life, you know," he said in rather strangled tones.

"Perhaps one day you'll do the same for me," said Jante. And smiled again.

# PART III
## Resistance

# Chapter 13

Training continued to advance for the group and Peredis, with his new found kinship with Jante, had made leaps and bounds in his progress. He saw changes in his physique which continued to give him confidence in his ability to carry out the task before him, finding his father's axe. Through his hard work and dedication he had also gained the respect and admiration of all his fellow recruits, and his progress greatly impressed his instructors

After carrying out another difficult orienteering exercise with the approval of both Sigmund and Stephane his confidence was soaring. That was until a few days later he was called into the office unexpectedly. These summons always made him feel nervous.

"We have a situation, Peredis," Sigmund began. "The Federal army has been very active in recent weeks on the

Outside," by which he meant beyond the boundaries of Eremore "and we have lost Aitor, an important resistance leader. We've been asked to provide a replacement. Both Stephane and myself believe you may be ready to join the movement where help is badly needed. It's a dangerous mission in the front line but we'll be sending Itxaso with you. She, as you know, is very capable, and she knows the terrain and the villages all along the mountain range."

Peredis had had little conversation so far with Itxaso who stayed mostly with Edurne and Rowena in their time off. She was a striking girl with snow-white complexion and jet black hair. Like her companions she was incredibly fit and outshone most of the others in competitive races and manual combat. Anton was especially taken by her, which gave rise to some teasing from Conor and Bar.

"When do we leave?" he asked.

"Tomorrow at first light," said Sigmund. "A guide will take you on horseback through one of the mountain passes, and then Itxaso will show you how to reach the eastern resistance camp where you'll be based. I will join you a little later for a mission I need to prepare in the upper valley."

"How long will we be deployed on the Outside?"

"Until our support tasks are completed. We'll receive instructions in due course. Any more questions? No. Get ready to leave tomorrow then."

*\*\*\**

The following morning as the sun tipped above the horizon, Itxaso and Peredis met outside the staff office. They nodded to each other but didn't speak. Itxaso led the way down a track in the woods where a guide was waiting with two saddled horses.

Most of that day was spent travelling into the mountains, going deeper and deeper by narrow stony paths where they had to dismount. A few times Itxaso let out a cry as she recognised a feature or a distant shepherd's croft. But the guide didn't alter his pace. Finally they began a descent which led them out of the shadow of the mountain and into a broad meadow where a shallow river ran. Here the guide stopped and turned.

"You know your way now," he said to Itxaso who grasped his hand in thanks. Peredis gave a gesture of farewell. He was entering a new world and it was the beginning of yet another big adventure in his life.

*** 

Life in the resistance camp high on a mountain slope was pleasant enough. There were about twelve members, men and women. They slept in caves and shelters dug out of the hillside and well hidden from the valley below. Their main task was to ambush Federal army convoys. Peredis felt happily engaged in this kind of warfare. It was basically the same as the training games they did on Gannet's Nest. Sigmund arrived unexpectedly one evening as the sun went down. He reported that a villager called Ander had been arrested by the Federals under suspicion of being a resistance fighter. The man, called Ander, was only an innocent farmer.

"If we mount up quickly we can rescue him," Sigmund said. "They'll be heading for the north end of the valley. I need a squad of four to intercept them with an extra horse." Itxaso and Peredis needed no more convincing. Within moments they were speeding down towards the valley road below. A few miles along the route they came to a pine forest which would give cover for the horses and provide an ambush. Added to which night was falling. They found a few logs to create an obstacle in the roadway and hid themselves in the bushes. Soon they could see the approaching lights of the Federal vehicle.

It was all over within five minutes. The Federals were seized and bound hand and foot by the side of the road. The farmer was released and given a horse to ride. Then the raiders disappeared into the hills.

"That was a perfect example of a raid," said Sigmund, as they returned to the base, pleased with himself and with the squad. "But the Federals are bound to come looking for Ander and his family again. We've got to get them away to safety. I'll organise an escape for them by sea, it's the best way. In the meantime they can hide in one of the barns in the valley. Itxaso, can you find them a secure hiding place for a couple of days?"

"Leave it to me," said Itxaso. True to her word she found a safe refuge for Ander and his little family until Sigmund turned up with transport, having organised the escape route down to the sea. It was no great distance to the sheltered cove where a boat waited offshore at anchor.

Itxaso and Peredis helped the family down to the water's edge. As they waited, a burly figure approached rowing an inflatable dinghy to the very edge of the rocks. Jumping on to shore, he held out a helping hand. In the gloom, Peredis thought he recognised the helper. He looked across at the anchored yacht ... and then he suddenly realised. The boat was the *Kresala*, the yacht that had once brought his mother and himself from Heimhaven, and their helpers were none other than Nestor and Gorka, the crew who had travelled with and fought alongside his father on the Day of Disaster.

"Where will you be taking them?" Peredis asked.

"Down to the southern border," came the reply. "Where the mountain meets the sea."

"Which mountain?"

"The Peak of Larroun."

"Then I need to go with you," Peredis said instantly. "Please, Gorka. Don't you recognise me? I'm Peredis, the son of Aenvar. Will you take us to the Peak of Larroun?"

The burly man peered more closely at the young man before him. "The son of Aenvar?" he said cautiously. Then his face lit up. "Yes, of course, Peredis! You've grown so much. I'll take you if Nestor agrees. We have to drop off the family near the Peak so it's a stone's throw away."

The last time Nestor and Gorka had seen Peredis, he was just a young boy. But as soon as he greeted them they understood who he was and there were embraces all around. Nestor agreed with Sigmund to take Peredis and Itxaso up to the mountain, understanding how important Larroun was.

Their craft glided away from the rocky coast and Nestor took them southwards keeping a good distance from the shore.

"We've never been back to Larroun," Gorka said bitterly. "The place has bad memories."

"But you know the Chieftain's axe disappeared?"

"Yes, of course. Without a trace. We managed to bring your father's body back to Heimhaven, but there was no sign of the axe."

"That's why we need to search the Peak. To see if we can find any sign of it."

"Aye," Gorka said, "for your father's sake I would gladly go on a search with you. He was a great man."

"And I would take you as close as I can to the shore," said Nestor. "I can anchor there and wait for you to climb the Peak."

As they came closer to the little harbour where the family would disembark and be taken to a safe destination, Peredis felt his heart beating with anticipation. Here the silhouette of the Peak soared above them as they came in close to shore. Bidding them farewell Nestor steered the *Kresala* away from the shore and round a peninsula where there was a quiet anchorage.

"We'll take the narrow track on the seaward side," Gorka said. "The ascent isn't difficult, and the battle area was about halfway towards the summit. Ready to go?" he asked, turning to Itxaso and Peredis. Both nodded agreement and got in the dinghy to row to shore.

The lower slope of the mountain was easy enough but the climb began to challenge them more. With the three of them advancing in line they covered a good part of the hilltop. Gorka, slightly ahead of the line stopped when he came to a slight dip up ahead and raised his hand as if to signal something. He called Peredis and Itxaso over and they went closer to see where he was staring at the ground.

"What is it, Gorka?" Peredis asked.

"This is the area," he said, "and there's something here which isn't normal."

Peredis and Itxaso approached further to see what was there. Gorka pointed downwards to the ground. There was a shape on the bare soil, clearly blackened by fire, a shape which looked like the double form of a cross.

"What do you think, Itxaso?" Gorka looked at them, querying with his glance.

"It's a burn mark, isn't it?" said the girl getting down low.

"What do you see, Itxaso?" Peredis asked.

"Smell it." Gorka said.

"It's foul, whatever it is," asserted Itxaso making a face.

"It's the same smell, what's left of it." Peredis looked anguished as he breathed in. It was what he had smelt in the tapestry but now much fainter, like a clinging residue. They studied the depression on the soil and tried to make sense of the scorched pattern. It was like nothing in nature. Then Itxaso bent near the ground to examine it. She let her finger touch the soil. Without warning, a gust of wind blew up a cloud of acrid fumes which almost blinded them and choked their lungs. Gorka and Peredis, caught unawares, reeled back, shielding their faces. In the same instant, the air was suddenly full of agonised cries, the noise of battle, screams of the dying and wounded. Then the noise passed as quickly as it had arrived.

Itxaso, who was standing closest, threw up her arms, gave a shrill cry and fell to the ground where she lay motionless.

"Peredis, see to Itxaso," Gorka said urgently as he checked around. "Make sure she's breathing."

Peredis crawled to the girl's side and checked her pulse. She was breathing steadily. He could see no sign of injury and thought it was more shock than anything else.

"I don't know what happened there, but we must get her back to the boat," said Gorka. "Can we manage between us?"

The journey back down the hill wasn't easy but they were able to support Itxaso between them and reach the *Kresala* where Nestor had her anchored.

"What on earth happened to her?" Nestor cried, seeing Itxaso's condition.

"We simply don't know," Gorka said, carrying Itxaso below deck. "It was as if she got a great shock and fainted. We need to revive her and keep her warm."

"And get back to the home village," said Nestor, "as fast as we can. She needs help."

Fortunately the transport that Sigmund had used to take the family down to the cove was still where they'd left it while waiting for their return from Larroun. As they arrived, villagers came out to help and sent for a doctor, while a child was dispatched to fetch Itxaso's cousin who lived in a farmhouse nearby. "We can't do much else for the moment," said Sigmund. "We'll come and check on her tomorrow."

First thing the next morning, Peredis and Sigmund rode down to the village to see how Itxaso was. It seemed she had recovered with all the care and attention in her cousin's home. They found her sitting up in bed and talking to Gorka and Nestor who were about to leave.

"We'll come back in a few days and check how you are," the seafarers said.

"I can't thank you enough for all you've done," said Itxaso.

Sigmund had a mission in the village, too, and went off to attend to it leaving Peredis on his own with Itxaso.

"I'll let you rest now," he said, "and come by later." He moved towards the door.

"No, Peredis," she called him back. "I have something to tell you and you alone." He went to sit beside her on a couch.

"What is it?" he asked.

"I don't know what happened to me on the mountain," she said, "but it was like a message, a vision."

"What about?" he leaned in closer.

"About your father's axe," she said. "So it's a message for you, too. It was a dream, and in the dream a woman spoke to me. I was going down a long tunnel towards a ball of fire, and the axe was in the fire. The voice said the axe must be redeemed by a woman pure of heart who will sacrifice herself. Then I was on the mountain where we were searching and there was a fierce struggle going on between good and evil. There were forces trying to help me up and other forces trying to stop me. I managed to stand upright and then I saw the fourfold axe in front of me. It was sending out a shaft of light to the horizon and across the ocean to the Winter Isles. You see what this means, don't you?"

"The axe is in Hvideland and we have to find the woman who will sacrifice herself and redeem the axe."

"But redeem? What does that mean? And who and where is the woman?"

"I don't know. Suppose it means you, yourself, Itxaso. Suppose you're the one who has to cross the ocean. It was your dream."

"I know. I need to follow this through, Peredis."

Even as she spoke, Peredis saw the cloud of doubt and puzzlement clearing from her eyes, and a new strength shone from them.

"And how will you get to the Winter Isles?" he asked, still struggling to understand her place in his destiny.

"Nestor will take me ... Won't he?" she said simply. "Who else?"

Peredis couldn't help laughing nervously. Probably because he was so afraid for her.

# Chapter 14

Gorka and Nestor returned after a week and were glad to see Itxaso up and about where she was staying with her cousin. Gorka said they had an important message for Peredis and needed to meet with Sigmund, too, but it would have to wait. The whole village seemed to be humming with one activity or another.

Waiting for news from Gorka and Sigmund was the hardest thing for Peredis at that time. At one point they went back down the coast to have a further look at the area below the Peak. As before, they came back disappointed.

Back in the village, Peredis watched Itxaso talking with Nestor and Gorka, and knew she was asking them to travel to Winter Isles, a major journey for them. Sigmund noticed it too.

"Do you think, Peredis," he began carefully, "that Gorka needs you to return to Hvideland as well?"

"No, no," he frowned in disbelief. "I'm not ready for that."

Sigmund nodded. "I understand. You're going to be needed in Europa. There are stirrings of rebellion all around the continent. The Vasconians see in you the bearer of your father's banner, his sword and shield, not to mention the Chieftain's axe. So who's ruling now in Hvideland?"

"My father's cousin, Ari, but he rules without true authority. He seized power after my father's death."

"Are you in danger from this Ari?" Sigmund inquired with a serious expression.

"I have the protection that my mother left me, but beyond that there's something evil that threatens me, I'm sure of it. My tutor Adhemar said I was only really safe at La Motte. He put a special protection around me there."

"La Motte? Your uncle's estate."

"Yes."

"I remember our discussion when you first arrived at Gannet's Nest.

You were immature, vulnerable, even disturbed. And though you've grown and matured, you're still vulnerable, even after all your Brigade training."

"Well, in spite of that it seems Gorka must have some mission for me. He said we need to meet on the *Kresala*. He has something important to show us."

"There's news from the south," Gorka began after they had assembled in the cabin of the *Kresala*. "First I bring greetings from the resistance in the southern states. It's not an exaggeration to say they're in the grip of an uprising. Their supporters are on the streets in huge numbers. The protests are growing daily in spite of the brutal crackdown of the armed police. Now the military are being deployed. Hundreds have been arrested. The prisons are full. There's even talk of executions. But with every arrest, every act of violence, the resistance adds to its ranks. The days of the dictators are numbered and the southern states want independence. To that end, the resistance leaders came together a week ago and signed a joint declaration to show how united they are for a common end."

Here Gorka reached down and opened a cupboard, taking out a red leather cylinder which he placed on the table.

"This is the sealed scroll of the declaration. They call it the Charter of Freedom," he said solemnly. "Each of the rebel states has signed up to it, as well as the Vasconians in exile, and they want our help now to take it to the resistance in the City. The Charter, once it's signed there, will aim to bring all the resistance groups together in the same way that Aenvar's Visionaries tried to do before their cruel defeat on the Day of Disaster. Therefore," here he paused and looked towards Peredis, "their great wish is for Peredis to carry the scroll to the City and deliver it."

There was a long silence at this point. Peredis was speechless, and it seemed the others were equally without words. Gorka was nodding encouragingly in his direction. Sigmund's expression gave nothing away.

Nestor took the round leather cylinder in both hands and held it towards Peredis.

"This declaration is what your father would have wanted," he said with passion. "It's what he fought for. It's his legacy to us all."

Sigmund broke his silence. "How do we know the City is ready for this?"

121

"We have contacts that Peredis will have to link up with to deliver the scroll. All the signs coming from those people indicate the City is on the edge of turmoil. The royal palace is in some disarray with talk of plots against the king himself, even involving the royal family. We've known this for some while but now the situation is becoming acute."

"So you think the time is right?" Sigmund was looking for reassurance.

"Absolutely," Nestor replied vigorously. "You have the evidence in front of you." He held up the scroll and placed it on the table between them. "This in itself is a sign of the times."

"I understand, perhaps more than anyone, why Peredis is important for this mission," Sigmund responded. His tone was firm and deliberate. "But Peredis is my right hand. I don't want to put him at risk or lose him to no purpose."

"It's his destiny," Nestor replied rather tersely. "What could be a greater purpose than that?"

"Then how do we ensure he reaches the City safely? And travelling at the tail end of summer. The weather will be changing."

"That's a good question," Peredis intervened for the first time. "I've never travelled beyond the mountains of the south and Eremore itself. How am I supposed to find my way to the City? And link up, as you say, with these folk you're connected with?"

"We'll find you a guide," Nestor said. "Surely," his question was directed at Sigmund, "we can find someone reliable locally?"

"Yes," Sigmund said thoughtfully, "we have just the man for that task, someone who's trained with Peredis and would be ideal. His name is Mikel."

Mikel was one of the Snakes but Peredis knew little about his background, only that he'd defected from the Federals a while back. He was a little older than the other recruits, as strong as a horse and quick to learn. But he was a taciturn fellow not given to conversation.

"Mikel grew up in the City," Sigmund went on. "He knows his way around, he's tough and reliable and trustworthy. If they both go, I'd miss them badly but Mikel would be a safe companion for Peredis and that's what matters here."

One important issue remained for Peredis.

"I'd like to go back home, to my uncle's, before making the journey to the City."

Nestor shook his head slowly. "I don't think that would be a good idea," he said. "This mission has to have the greatest secrecy and you must always keep under cover. Your uncle's estate might be under surveillance or even raided at any time."

Sigmund agreed with him. "One mistake might expose your whole mission to danger. And suppose you were captured and the Charter was taken. It would expose all those who had signed it to danger as well."

Regretfully Peredis had to accept what they were saying.

"What do you think, Gorka?" they asked.

"I agree with Nestor," he replied, leaning across the table and offering Peredis the cylinder. "This task is meant for you, Peredis."

"Then I must accept it," he said, taking the leather cylinder from Gorka and feeling the terrible weight of it in his hands.

Nestor spoke. "In the City you must find a man called Isander Venizelos and deliver the Charter to him. He runs an underground network of dissidents, most of them originally from the southern states. These people are all well connected through family and tribal loyalties and they'll be important elements in the new Europa when it comes."

"The new Europa?" Peredis expressed surprise. "Do you see it? Already?"

"I see it as clearly as I see you," Nestor said with conviction. "The forging of the new Europa is simply a matter of time. And you'll be a part of it, I can assure you, Peredis. An important part."

Those words were to echo in his mind and heart for a long time to come

# Chapter 15

His first view of the City ... it was like arriving on another planet. It literally took his breath away. Peredis had always seen the Citadel of Eremore as the loveliest of cities, and it never failed to impress as you arrived there. But as Mikel and himself came over the last brow of the pass opening up to the City's seething and soaring immensity of towers and fly-overs, crowded esplanades and airways with airpod traffic buzzing in all directions .... well, here was a new world beyond anything he had ever imagined. Vast and overwhelming, it stretched to the far horizon. At its heart, great avenues led off from a central square where a mighty stone building soared skywards with arches and spires so fine you wondered how it stayed aloft.

Mikel laughed out loud as he saw the expression on his companion's face. Their long journey riding together in sometimes wintry conditions through the endless forests of the continent had brought them closer together and Peredis discovered that, once he'd learned to relax with his companion, Mikel had quite a sense of humour.

"That's the Rational Reform Cathedral," he said. "Beautiful, isn't it? Though of course it belongs to another epoch in history. It must be a thousand years old and miraculously still standing. Then further away," here he pointed to the far side of the City where a palatial structure stood in parkland with another huge square before it, "that's a newer creation altogether, the royal palace."

"It's stunning, isn't it!" Peredis exclaimed.

"It's an extraordinary building," Mikel agreed. "You'd never guess it's a virtual structure."

Peredis looked at him, puzzled. "Virtual structure? What do you mean?"

"It's not real. Well, of course, it is real but not in a traditional sense. It's a high plasticity construction."

"Explain what that means, Mikel, you've lost me."

"High plasticity is a modern high-tech creation, a spin-off of the space exploration program. It's managed by SEPTIMUS. Technically it's amazing. They say people who live inside, the royal family mainly, that is, really think they're living in the eighteenth century."

"SEPTIMUS, you said? What on earth is that?" Now he was even more confused.

"Supreme European Palace Timespace Unity Set. Probably one of the greatest technical achievements of the last century and the cornerstone of the new Europus. If only we could get in there and blow it up, most of our problems would be solved."

He grinned as he saw Peredis' utter lack of understanding. "You've had a sheltered life, haven't you, Peredis?"

He nodded, his head still reeling. "I guess I have a lot to learn about the modern world."

"Well, I'm no expert," Mikel said, "but I think I know more than you, so at least I can tell you the little that I know."

"Please fill me in because I'm totally out of my depth. People here are going to think I'm an ignorant peasant."

"Shall we start on page one, then?"

"You mentioned something called the space exploration program ...?"

As they went along, Mikel started to tell Peredis some of the basics. He was surprised at his companion's total ignorance of the twenty-third century. Peredis was fairly surprised himself, listening to his account. Life at La Motte and in Eremore hadn't prepared him in the slightest for this amazing new world so different from anything he had ever experienced.

Their first task on arriving in the City would be to locate some of the contacts that Nestor had mentioned to them. But before that they looked for a place to stay on the edge of town where they could also stable the horses. This was their first night of sleeping indoors after their long journey and a good meal and a soft bed were comforts that were more than welcome. As Peredis had done ever since it was entrusted to him, he slept with the Charter in its red leather cylinder clutched tightly in his grasp.

The following day after a welcome breakfast of eggs and toasted bread, the two started their search in earnest for the mysterious Isander Venizelos, the name of their main contact. Mikel said he had a friend, Andrew, who was a journalist and well informed about people and events. They should try to locate him at his newspaper office which was downtown on Cathedral square. They left the lodging and, setting off on foot, joined the throng of people streaming in all directions. It took them a while to get used to the sheer numbers surrounding them. But Mikel seemed in his element and very quickly guided them to moving walkways which they could hop on and off. Above them, airpods flew almost silently along their own separate flyways between the soaring tower blocks.

As they walked Peredis could see Mikel becoming more and more concerned.

"What's the matter?" he asked.

Mikel made a face. "Can't you see people looking at us? And those airpods above us watching everything, all police and Feds, by the way. Public traffic is only allowed at ground level. We're attracting attention."

He was right. They had dressed in plain simple clothes for the journey so as not to attract attention, but here their style of dress stood out like a sore thumb.

"It's horrendous," said Mikel. "We look like southern terrorists. We need to go down to the shopping level. Follow me."

So saying, he stepped off the walkway carrying them and took a stairway down to a street level below. They entered a huge hall where acres of glass offered displays of every product under the sun and my companion quickly found what he was looking for. Twenty minutes later, dressed in neat inconspicuous outfits, they left the hall and returned to the upper walkway which carried us to Cathedral square. Then they crossed over to a three storey building opposite which a large sign announced as the offices of City News. An elevator took them to the main floor.

Mikel scanned the department lists for the name of his friend Andrew.

"He's not listed here," he said. "I'll have to ask around on the news floor. Will you wait here a moment?" He pushed open the glass doors that led to a large office area and Peredis saw him go up to the nearest person. An animated conversation followed. Peredis could see Mikel looking upset after which the other became more and more agitated until he summoned a colleague from another desk close by. The newcomer seemed to be telling Mikel to leave, and took his arm forcefully to guide him to the door. Mikel pushed him off as he came away but then at the last moment the other leaned close and whispered something before he withdrew.

"Bad news," Mikel said on rejoining the walkway. "Andrew doesn't work here any more. They say he had to leave because of some articles he wrote. His colleague said he was getting letters threatening his life."

"Do they know where he is?"

"They didn't want to say exactly, but he may have taken refuge in the mountains."

"That sounds like a really serious threat, then," said Peredis, looking back at the news floor.

"Absolutely. The first man I spoke to was really nervous. Didn't want to talk about it. Then when I asked if he knew Venizelos he clammed up. Wouldn't say another word and called his boss over."

"Did he explain why?"

"No, he just looked really scared. Kept looking around as if he was afraid to be seen talking to us."

"But then the second guy must have said something useful. At the end, I mean, didn't he say something to you."

"Yes, he whispered a name, then told me to take care."

"What name?"

"Kellsberg."

"Who on earth is that?"

"Don't know, but seems he's dangerous."

"Very helpful," Peredis said, sighing. "Where do we go now?"

Mikel was frowning as they took the elevator back to the square. "Don't you think there's something strange going on here?"

"What do you mean?"

"I don't know. I get the feeling that things are a bit tense. There's something in the air and I don't like the feel of it."

Almost on cue, as they walked out on to the square they began to notice people streaming past the Cathedral and down the broad avenue that led to the royal palace. Everyone was going in the same direction. Mikel gave an inquiring look. "Shall we take a look?"

"Yes," Peredis responded instantly. "Let's see what's going on."

The crowds became more and more dense as they joined the throng and progressed down the central avenue. There was an air of excitement all around with people of all ages, shapes and sizes. Children were tugging their parents along as if to hurry them.

"What's all the fuss about?" Mikel asked someone close by.

"The royal family, of course. It's their Anniversary," came the reply.

Mikel looked across at Peredis and shrugged. He clearly had no idea what that was, having grown up in a City without royalty in his day. The two weren't made much wiser as they entered the great square before the palace and stood waiting along with tens of thousands of others already assembled. They could see little except the main facade of the building behind tall gilt railings. Something was about to happen but they had no idea what it might be. They didn't have long to wait. From the far side a brass band struck up and immediately the crowd stirred with a growing hum of excitement. It seemed there was movement and Peredis glimpsed an arrival of colour on the central balcony of the palace facade. At this the atmosphere in the square exploded with excitement, red and white flags began waving all around the immense esplanade and deafening cheers sounded to the skies. Now they could see a group standing on the balcony. It had to be the royal family, though all they could see from their vantage point was a series of coloured blobs. All the same, Peredis felt a thrill in his chest that was new for him. Even though he grew up around royals, this was the first time he felt truly in awe of a single group of people. How could he possibly know his life was so soon to change, and change utterly.

A sign that something was wrong happened only moments later when he was shoved aside as two men in dark suits suddenly slid through the mass of people and seized an individual nearby. They dragged him away, almost knocking Peredis over as they went. He was about to protest but looking around the crowd he began to notice other men in suits circulating as if searching for something or someone, then again suddenly seizing on an individual and leading them off.

"What's all this about?" Peredis questioned Mikel. "Who are they after?"

"A mystery," said Mikel, shaking his head. The only small clue, which seemed insignifiant, was when they noticed that all the individuals taken away had a green ribbon pinned to their jackets.

The two also noticed that watching the crowds from above, on the roof of every building, were armed police or soldiers who looked as if they meant business.

Things became clearer later on as they went to find lunch in a bar. They came to a place that served a splendid meal, green peppers tossed in oil, a lamb stew with rich gravy and slices of delicious cheese to end with. They thought that whatever else was wrong with the City, the food was excellent.

As the landlord served them at table, they innocently asked what it meant to wear a green ribbon. The man reacted as if he'd been shot, and made an urgent sign not to speak. It was the scene at the newspaper office repeating itself. As they were about to leave the restaurant, the landlord drew them into a corridor leading to the back of the bar, saying, "You aren't from around here, are you, mister?"

"No," Peredis replied. "Not exactly." He was intrigued. No on had ever called him mister before.

"Don't talk about the green ribbons," came the advice, "or you'll end up in a police cell."

"But who are they? What do they want?"

"Heretics," he said in a low voice.

"Heretics?" Peredis was none the wiser but thought it best not to pursue the question. "Thanks for the tip." he replied casually. They turned to leave and were moving towards the door when he called after them.

"Wait."

He approached Mikel and said something in a tongue that Peredis didn't recognise. Mikel's hand went up to a little round emblem that he wore on a cord around his neck. Peredis had never asked what it was, though he'd seen that Gorka wore a similar cross.

"The four be with you," the man murmured.

"And with you," murmured Mikel.

They clasped hands briefly as Peredis watched with some puzzlement at this sudden turn of events. Instinctively his hand went under his jacket to touch the leather cylinder.

"I can tell you're on a mission," the landlord said. "Who are you searching for?"

"One called Venizelos," Mikel said. "He's hard to find."

"Not if you know the way," came the reply. "Will he know you?"

"He's expecting us," Mikel said.

"Then I will tell you the way."

He reached into a drawer under the bar and took out a coin which he gave to Mikel.

"Go north out of town through the woods on the far slope. You will come to a black tower. Ask for Jack the Woodsman and give him this coin. He'll take you to Venizelos."

"We're travelling on horseback," Peredis said.

"Then you don't even need to go through the City. Ride around the parkland beyond the palace until you reach a big circle of oak trees. From there you'll see a kind of summerhouse with columns near the edge of the woods. Take the bridle path from there that heads towards the northern hills. You'll see the black tower in the distance. You can't miss it. It's quite a landmark. Just make sure you're not followed. Watch the skies, too, in case of drones. You can shelter in the woods until the coast is clear. And, by the way, best to hide that *lauburu* round your neck. You don't want to be picked off the streets for wearing that."

"Do you trust that barman?" Peredis asked Mikel later as they rode along the tracks of the royal parkland.

"I do," he said.

"What made him call you back? Did he recognise your little pendant?"

"Yes. It showed him I'm a Vasconian."

"He mentioned its name. Tell me what it is exactly."

"It's a *lauburu*, a Vasconian cross, very ancient, and its arms symbolise the four elements, water, earth, air and fire. The whole circle represents the sun. We wear it for protection."

"Apparently it won't protect you if you get arrested," Peredis said, smiling.

Mikel laughed. "I knew he was Vasconian anyway."

"How come?"

"That delicious meal. Mmm," he sighed deeply. "Took me straight back to home."

"Pity, then, we can't risk going back to that bar."

"Mr Venizelos, whoever he is, clearly isn't Vasconian. Not with a name like that."

"So no decent meals from him. That's a shame."

"You never know. Could be Greek," Mikel suggested. "They like decent food, don't they?"

"You're making me hungry again, just talking about it."

They were leaving the royal palace to their left as they went along, then crossing the parkland past the ring of massive oak trees that the barman had mentioned. From here the summer house was clearly visible and they continued on their way towards the rising ground which led to the woods. As they reached the treeline they stopped and looked back to ensure that no one was following. But the view of the palace from this vantage point took their breath away, with the beautiful stonework of the facade arranging before them its multiple ranks of windows and decorative features.

"It's magnificent, isn't it?" Mikel said with awe in his voice.

"It is indeed," Peredis agreed. "But this high plasticity idea is really beyond my understanding."

"Never mind the technology," Mikel said, "just admire the results."

And so they did. Then, following the barman's advice, they glanced skywards to make sure that no spy drones were watching them. The sky was a perfect canopy of blue above.

"The sky, as well, is part of the technology, apparently," Mikel pointed out. "They order up the weather as and when they want it."

"Incredible," Peredis said. "What about that black spot, though? Did they order that up?" Something had caught his attention which seemed less than perfect. It was a number of small dense black clouds hovering above the palace and casting a shadow on the perfect landscape.

"I've heard they do get technical problems sometimes, not surprising, like any major software. But that patch up there just looks like a storm cloud," Mikel said. "Like we get in the mountains."

"Yes, similar," Peredis responded, "but strangely dark, don't you think?"

"Maybe," he admitted. "It does look rather menacing. Best we get going. Don't want to be caught in a storm."

So saying, they spurred their horses onwards and took the bridle path that led up the slope into the woods. After thirty minutes or so they could see smoke rising above the trees in the distance and the silhouette of the black tower. Very soon they arrived in a clearing where there were signs of human activity. On one side stood the stone-built tower which had the air of a look-out. In the central area was a large dome of smouldering timbers. They looked around but could see nobody in sight. Then a voice came from above. "Who are you? What do you want?"

The voice came from the top of the tower where the speaker, whoever it was, remained hidden.

"We seek Jack the Woodsman," Mikel called up as the two dismounted. "We have something for him."

"Jack the Woodsman needs nothing," came the reply.

"We were told to give him this coin," Mikel added, showing the metal disc.

"Jack the Woodsman needs no coin."

"But this is a special coin," Peredis said, examining it more closely for the first time. On one face it had a sun, on the other face a single word.

"It has writing on it, a name perhaps," he guessed.

"What name is that?"

"Mari, M-A-R-I," he spelled it out.

Silence followed from above. They heard the clattering of wooden clogs coming down the inside of the tower and an extraordinary figure emerged from a doorway at the bottom. Wild and shaggy were the only words to describe him. He was small but wiry, and clad in sheepskins from head to toe. His face was hardly visible with the unkempt russet hair and beard that covered it, escaping from under a broad black beret. But his eyes were sharp and brilliant, keen to examine us closely.

"What does Mari ask of Jack the Woodsman?"

"The way to Venizelos."

Peredis held out the coin which he took in his hand and checked briefly before tucking it in the band of his flat beret.

"Have you seen the cloud?" he asked suddenly, looking agitated.

Mikel and his companion looked at each other, rather puzzled, then it dawned on them.

"You mean the black cloud over the palace?"

"Mari is angry," came the response.

"Yes," they agreed carefully. "It looks angry, that cloud."

"Who sent you? What do you want?" the little man inquired again, screwing up his eyes a bit to see them better.

"We're seeking Isander Venizelos," Mikel replied.

The little man stared unblinking at the ground for a few moments as if processing our request. Then he sprang into action.

"We must hurry. Mari is angry." He turned and scurried away across the clearing, then stopped and looked back. "We must hurry," he repeated. "Hurry!"

Holding their horses' bridles they set off after him as he ducked and dived between the trees going deeper and deeper into the forest but always at a run, forcing them to trot after him. They had absolutely no idea where they were going. Every so often the little man seemed doubtful himself as he stopped more than once and asked, "Venizelos?"

"Yes, Venizelos," they confirmed.

"Not Wildern?"

"No, not Wildern..." Wherever or whoever that was.

It was with some relief that they eventually arrived at a proper path or road which showed signs of traffic. Here their guide stopped and pointed to their left.

"Venizelos. Two miles. Maybe three. Take care." At this he made a gesture as if holding a gun. Then without another word he ducked back into the trees and left them standing there by the side of the road.

The two mounted their horses and took the direction he'd indicated, somewhat cautiously given his warning. Sure enough, in a couple of miles as they rounded a bend they were faced with a closed gateway into an estate. Two armed men emerged from a sentry post and signalled them to stop.

"What's your business?" one of them challenged, raising his firearm threateningly.

"We have a message for Isander Venizelos," Peredis called back.

"Say what it is."

"It's for his eyes only," Mikel replied.

"Mr Venizelos doesn't take messages. Turn around and go away."

"He'll take this message. It's important. It's from the south. Speak to him on your radio. Tell him the son of Aenvar is here. He'll be very upset with you if you send us away."

The two conferred, then one of them went into the sentry post, obviously to check what they should do. He came back straightaway.

"You can pass," he said grimly, going to open and push back the gate.

"Is it far to the house?" Mikel asked.

"You'll see," came the curt reply. "Stay on the driveway."

"Charming folk, aren't they!" Mikel commented as they progressed along the road which ran between neat vineyards and slopes of walnut and cherry trees as far as the eye could see.

Peredis too was taken aback by the reception they'd had. "Looks as if this Mr Venizelos has weight around here."

"Let's hope he's friendlier than his men." Mikel pulled a face.

"Well, he recognised who I was, so that's a good start."

"I do hope so," Mikel said. "Because if we fall out with these fellows, I don't think we'll leave here alive."

"Thanks for that encouraging thought," Peredis said, laughing. But he shared Mikel's concern. They had wandered like lambs into a situation over which they had no control at all. Who was this man Venizelos? What kind of a person needed such tight security? Peredis asked himself. He was about to find out.

# Chapter 16

Isander Venizelos was nothing like expected. As they rode up to the elegant ranch-style house which overlooked his extensive lands, the man himself, tall, with an aristocratic air about him, came down the steps to greet them. As they dismounted, he shook them both warmly by the hand.

"We've been expecting you," he said. "It's a privilege to know the son of Aenvar. Your father was one of my youthful heroes."

He went to welcome Mikel. "I know your story, Mikel. I admire your action in crossing over from the Federals. It made waves here at the time and I know it was difficult for your family." He clapped him on the shoulder. "I did some crossing over of my own at one stage, so I know what it's like. But more of that later."

Isander Venizelos was a big man, strong of build and bald headed. He had a forceful manner about him which was quite forbidding and you could tell he was a leader, used to being obeyed. But he had a kindly and respectful side to him which was less expected and which for Peredis, at least, only added to his authority. His manner was certainly a big contrast to the gorillas at the gate.

Venizelos signalled to someone who appeared from the side of the house. "Look after the horses," he instructed. "We won't be needing them again today."

He turned towards his guests. "I'm only too pleased to welcome you, and hope you'll stay and enjoy our hospitality after your long journey."

As he led them indoors he leant over and whispered, "Do you have it?"

Peredis knew at once what he meant. He patted his jacket where he kept the leather cylinder close to him. "I have it," he said reassuringly.

"Then the first thing we must do is to put it somewhere safe. Mikel, will you wait for us here a moment or two?"

He took Peredis down a corridor and into a back room which looked more like a laundry than anything else, full of machines for heating, washing and drying. He went to one of the machines which had every appearance of a dryer but after opening its outer door, he put his hand inside and must have flipped a switch. The internal drum of the machine spun around and revealed a safe door. He entered a code and then looked towards Peredis.

"Are you happy for me to take charge of it?" he asked, smiling.

"Of course," said Peredis. "That's why I'm here."

"But you know the time isn't right yet ..."

"You're the best judge of that, Mr Venizelos."

"Call me Sander ..."

"Sander."

"When the time is right, Peredis, we'll come back here and open the Charter. Both of us, together. That will be the time to announce it. Agreed?"

"Agreed."

Peredis took off his jacket and slipped the cord of the leather cylinder over his head.

"It's sealed," he said.

"And will remain sealed, until we open it together." He handed Peredis a copper key and at the same time showed him a similar disc which slotted into the other. "You see? The key only works when the two pieces slide together. We each keep a half."

The cylinder was placed in the safe, and the door was secured again. There was a ceremonial clasping of hands.

"By the way," Sander said, tapping the machine, "this safe is earthquake and flood proof and fire proof. It can't be forced with explosives. Whatever is inside it will never be destroyed. When I put it in lockdown it descends to a cavity underground and is completely hidden until its appointed time, even to the end of time."

"I'm reassured," Peredis said laughingly. "But I sincerely hope I'm not around for the end of time."

"Nor me," his host took Peredis by the arm. "Now you and Mikel must relax and freshen up after your journey, and we'll meet up for dinner. Maia will show you your rooms."

The girl called Maia was waiting with Mikel for them to return and she invited them to follow her to the upper floor.

"You'll hear the gong for dinner," she said after showing them their rooms. "Ring the bell on your bedside table should you need anything. I've put clean clothes and towels for you."

"Speaking of the end of time ..."

They were relaxing in a comfortable sitting room after a delicious meal of oven baked fish with savoury rice, washed down with glasses of tart white wine. Now music played in the background and the glass of aromatic brandy that Peredis was warming in his hands was sending him to sleep. But Venizelos' words brought him back to earth.

"I was joking," Peredis said, only half-aware of what he meant.

"Of course." Their host gave a deep chuckle. "But actually I wasn't thinking of the entire universe but rather the threat to my grape harvest. We've had some nasty storms recently and to be honest I'm a little anxious."

"We did see a really threatening cloud as we came away from the royal palace."

"That's how it starts, that's right," Venizelos commented. "First the black cloud, then we get a really violent storm which doesn't last but is quite severe. What's curious about it, of course, is that the weather is controlled by SEPTIMUS. You know what that is, I guess."

"I explained it to Peredis," Mikel said, "as much as I know myself."

"Well, the palace in itself is an experiment in what they call high plasticity."

"Yes, Mikel mentioned that, whatever it is."

"It's a form of construction designed for space colonies when the time comes. The idea is to develop models which can self-organise once they're established on other planetary bodies. This is where it's so clever. The material itself is indestructible and once its objectives are programmed in, the 3-D model takes over. It needs vigilance, obviously, and maintenance, but the day-to-day reality that it creates pursues its own stable path. It's a total three dimensional virtual reality."

"Which means that it's real but not real," Mikel chipped in.

"Exactly."

"So what's the problem that you see?" Peredis asked.

"These weather patterns are the problem. They concern me. They shouldn't exist. I'm very much afraid they're symptoms of instability. The severe storms we've experienced recently should never affect us here like they have. They emanate from SEPTIMUS as if they were some form of escaping energy. So on one level I'm worried about my grape harvest. On another level, without wanting to be too dramatic, I'm worried, yes, about the end of the world as we know it ..."

He fell silent and they pondered his words without speaking.

"That's really serious, then," said Peredis. "And you're not joking?"

"I'm not joking, no. Not at all."

"So what could happen if the system collapses?" Mikel asked.

Venizelos gave a blank stare and shrugged his shoulders.

"Nobody knows," he said. "We'd be in a completely unknown dimension."

A sudden thought occurred to Peredis.

"What about the people living inside the system?"

"Yes," Mikel picked up the question. "The king, the royal family and so on. There are five children, aren't there? What do we know about them?"

"Yes, three girls and two boys. Charm, the eldest daughter, then Dream, then Emerald. And the boys Fion and Gentil. Fion is the successor to the throne."

"What happens to them?"

"We simply don't know," came the reply. "We can only hope they'd be rescued in time to escape the worst of it."

"So it really could be the end of the world. The world that we know, anyway."

"That's what we have to work with," he said. "As the old Chinese saying goes, a time of crisis is a time of opportunity. If the old order collapses, it'll be up to us to create a new order. That's where the Charter comes in. A new Charter for a new world."

"Then the end of Europus as well, surely." Peredis tried to absorb the idea and found it too overwhelming. The dream that his father and the Visionaries had fought and died for could become reality. It seemed like pure fantasy.

He could hardly sleep that night for all that was buzzing around in his head.

He woke with a start as he heard the roar of an engine outside and, leaping out of bed, he arrived at the window just in time to see their host accelerating away down the driveway on a powerful motorbike.

By the time he returned fifteen minutes later, Peredis was up, showered and dressed and had gone outside to look around the property. Maia had joined him and was showing him parts of the garden. He took the opportunity to find out more about her. She said she was a student and had taken on the job as a housekeeper and general help to get through her studies. Peredis deduced that Venizelos normally lived alone on this vast estate but didn't inquire further as to their relationship.

They went in to breakfast together with their host bringing fresh bread which he had bought locally. He looked troubled and Peredis asked him if he had any news from the City.

"I didn't go all the way into town," he said. "But I'm really worried about the weather situation. The sky is more and more menacing, a kind of brooding muddy colour with these black spots gathering. Very strange. We'll travel in this morning and see how things are developing. We can go in the estate pick-up so long as we stay off Federal roads."

Peredis had already noticed the sky darkening as he walked outside with Maia. By the time they were ready to leave for town, the entire dome of the sky had taken on a peculiar tone of muddy orange which barely allowed the sun to shine through.

"This is very strange," Venizelos shook his head as he drove down towards the gate. He stopped and spoke to his guards as they passed, telling them to be extra vigilant. Then he set off on the cart track which they had ridden along the day before to reach the estate.

"You might wonder why I have guards on my gate," he said as they sped towards the City. "It's a long story. Let's just say I fell out with some remarkably nasty people a few years back. Coming from the south, you've probably heard of them. Decadians, they call themselves. They've fortified themselves in the mountains down there, a long way off, but even so I have to be careful."

"We certainly do know them," Mikel and Peredis spoke at the same time. "We had a nasty brush with them recently and one of our team was killed."

"I'm very sorry to hear that," Venizelos frowned. "I'll tell you some time how I came to fall out with them ..." He fell silent and continued driving at a fair pace.

"Tell us about the little man in the woods," said Peredis. "He kept saying, Mari is angry, Mari is angry. I have no idea what he meant."

"Does he live in the forest, in that tower?" Mikel wanted to know. "And what is he burning there?"

"Jack the Woodsman? Yes, he lives in the forest and makes charcoal. That's what you saw burning. He's very shy and a bit odd, but harmless. You'll have noticed that he runs everywhere."

"Yes, we noticed," Peredis laughed. "We could scarcely keep up with him."

"I take him provisions about once a month," Venizelos said. "And I buy his charcoal of course." He was silent again for a moment. "So he told you Mari is angry?" he went on.

"That's what he kept saying."

"Mari is the sun, the spirit that gives life to the earth. So Mari is angry. Well," he added, gesturing to the sky. "It's certainly starting to look like it."

It was not long before he pulled off the road and drove through the trees until they came to a vantage point on a rise overlooking the City with the palace standing in its parkland below them. Here the morbid orange glow of the sky was even more noticeable but much more alarming was the sheer number of black clump-like storm clouds that cast a ghastly shadow over the whole area.

"Can you feel it?" Venizelos said. He opened the door of the vehicle, got out and stood on the ground. "There's a tremor in the earth. Like an earthquake."

Peredis and Mikel followed him. "It's in the air, too," said Peredis. "A kind of thrumming. I can feel it right through my body."

Even as they watched, the black spots began to form a solid canopy and the whole sky then entered some kind of transformation. Charged points of sparks began to flow earthwards like drops of rain, but coloured rain, red, gold and green, which fell on to the palace building and seemed to make it totally fluid. The shaking of the building could be felt even as far away as their vantage point.

"Dear heaven," Venizelos exclaimed. "What on earth is happening?" All three of them instinctively grasped the side of the vehicle to steady themselves.

The next minute they could see only too clearly what was happening. The palace started to metamorphose like a butterfly coming out of a chrysalis.

"SEPTIMUS has gone mad," Venizelos uttered, his voice full of alarm.

As they watched, the palace became almost liquid and twisted itself into a variety of architectural forms, one after the other, some recognisable, some never before seen. SEPTIMUS, apparently freed from his restraints, was putting on a spectacular show. And at the end of this display which must have gone on for some fifteen minutes, the result was simply magical. The liquid heart of the building rose in a mighty crown of elegant ribs, like drops of milk on a saucer, and opened itself up completely to the rainbow sky. But even then the show wasn't over. Now the Sun and the

Moon joined in the dance, coming closer and closer to each other, then descending to meld in the open cup of the building before rising and separating again, each on its own path towards opposite horizons. The sky became calm at last, misty with a brilliant sunlight that was almost unbearable to look at. But then, in a final shuddering of the earth, the whole area of the surrounding grassland began to shoot and grow until the palace was entirely trapped in an impenetrable tangle of vegetation. Only the tips of its lovely white crown remained visible above the newly grown forest.

Everyone stood there stunned and silent. They couldn't utter a single word. Before their very eyes, SEPTIMUS had created something of exquisite beauty. The only worry was that all this had taken place, so it seemed, without a single thought for the people of this earth. SEPTIMUS had taken over his world, and now it was completely outside their control.

Where did that leave the people?

# Chapter 17

Mikel and Peredis reined in their horses on the brow of the pass. Before them they could see the chain of the southern hills stretching from east to west like a great barrier across the continent. They were at a crossroads but, as elsewhere in the hills, there were no signs because the resistance had taken them down, literally to confuse the enemy.

"This is where our paths separate," Peredis said to his companion. "It's been a tremendous adventure, hasn't it, Mikel! My greetings to Sigmund and the Snakes."

They clasped hands in farewell. Mikel's path would lead him westwards towards the rolling hills of Vasconia and the ocean. Peredis' took him to La Motte, his home since childhood, near the deep glacial valleys of the south.

He knew only too well the sheer delight of that final leg of the journey home, following the river up to its crossing, then taking the path that leads into the peaceful valley of the estate. And he was especially excited this time. He was longing to see his uncle Robert, but not only that, he had quite a story to tell. It seemed an age since he'd left home and here he was returning a different man, stronger and, one hoped, a little bit wiser.

It was a wonderful homecoming as he rode up the slope to the house and saw Robert was already there, working in the wine press with the grape pickers.

"I wasn't expecting you yet," he cried, greeting Peredis with a warm embrace as the dogs, Oliver and Orlando, bounced around, joining their voices to the welcome. "You should have warned me you were on your way."

"I'm sorry, Robert," Peredis said. "Too much has been happening and I couldn't get a message to you. You must have heard the news from the City, the collapse of the royal palace."

"Rumours, rumours," he said. "Nothing that sounded remotely believable. The palace transforming, or some such fairy tale. The government in chaos and the royal family all dead? All we have here is rumours. Tell me the fine details once you've settled in."

Peredis went to stable his horse.

"Ximista will be pleased to be home again," Robert called out after him. "I've missed him."

And he was indeed pleased to see Robert, as he greeted him with his great soft nose. What joy for Ximista to be reunited with him. "Don't you worry," Robert said, stroking his mane as he tossed his head with pleasure. "Tomorrow we'll go for a good run."

As Peredis went indoors to bathe and change Robert called out: "I forgot to say. Adhemar arrives tomorrow morning. Somehow he knew you were heading home."

That was no surprise to Peredis at all.


All was in its customary place. The logs crackling in the great fireplace. The dogs warming themselves lazily by the hearth. Robert pensively sipping the red wine from the previous year, no doubt comparing it on his palate with the first pressing that day of the new harvest.

"It was really thoughtful of you to arrive in time for the grape picking." Those were Robert's first words when Peredis joined him in the salon. He had a twinkle in his eye as he spoke.

Peredis laughed. "Of course I'll help, as I always have. It wouldn't be La Motte without a dose of sweat and labour in the vineyards."

"First thing in the morning, then. As for the news, shall we wait till Adhemar gets here, for the full story?"

"That might be best, yes. There's a lot to tell."

"We've had such good accounts of you from Eremore, with Sigmund reporting back on your progress in Vasconia. You're starting to become a bit of a legend."

"Let's not exaggerate, Robert. I've just been doing my job, carrying out the tasks given to me. I have to say, though, the highlight was my mission to the City. With Mikel, of course, my comrade in arms from Vasconia. I couldn't have done it without him. But more of all that when Adhemar is here. I'm just so pleased he's coming."

Adhemar arrived as expected while Peredis was already out riding Ximista. He knew every path and trail and was completely sure footed as they raced around the estate and up to the ridge beyond.

From there the view, as always, was immense and splendid. On the farthest horizon he could just make out the twin horns of Mount Diabolus and the white mistiness of the Great Glacier. Eremore was somewhere beyond there, in another dimension. He knew he'd return there one day but for now it seemed that the most important tasks that faced him would be on the Outside. Events in the City had thrown everything into disorder and he wasn't at all sure what part he could play from now on. Thank goodness, he thought, Adhemar is on his way and he, at least, will be able to throw some light on what he should do next.

But he was a little nervous, too. Adhemar had found out about his trip to the Peak of Larroun, something he'd specifically told him not to do, and Peredis had ignored his advice. What would he have to say about that?

He didn't have to wait long to find out.

# Chapter 18

"It was a serious mistake." Adhemar spoke softly and firmly but there was no doubt he was giving Peredis a good ticking off. "I warned you of the evil in the place. You could have been attacked and deeply wounded. Look what happened to Itxaso. Worst of all, you led others into great danger."

They were sitting on a bench at the foot of his tower, where Adhemar stayed during his visits. At his side, Peredis felt like a small boy again, being punished, and couldn't meet his gaze.

"However," he went on, "that's all behind us now and you've redeemed yourself somewhat with your mission to the City."

The atmosphere relaxed, and Peredis breathed again.

"Did you meet Venizelos himself?"

"Yes, we did," he replied. "He was very welcoming.

He took charge of the Charter and put it in a safe place. He said when the time came, we'd open it together."

Adhemar nodded. "Good. That's all as it should be."

"Tell me about this Charter," Peredis said, frowning. "Although I was asked to deliver it, I still haven't got a clue what it is. Venizelos didn't tell me anything in the short time we were there."

Adhemar took out his pipe and started to fill it slowly from his green tobacco pouch.

"The Charter of Freedom is a very ancient document. It originated centuries ago in a temple in Graecia, far to the south and across the inner sea. It's a text written on parchment, a contract, if you like, a sort of blueprint for society. It was considered so sacred and important that it had a temple built to house it. Later in the wars of the inner sea the temple was sacked by invaders and the Charter was lost. It was thought to have perished because the invaders themselves had no respect for it. It was discovered, though, from researches in the last century, that the Charter survived and was taken across the inner sea for safekeeping to a monastery on a mountain. Which monastery and its whereabouts were unknown at first, but then coded instructions were discovered on a tomb in Mont Pietat, a monastery in the southern mountains. Before the search could go further, the house was assaulted during the War of Delusion and taken over by the Decadians, a godless movement known as the Reds."

"Yes, I know them only too well. We ran into them in Vasconia and I lost one of my team in the shoot-out. Sigmund said they were extremely dangerous."

"True enough," said Adhemar. "They mainly deploy in the area around the Great Glacier where the monastery is situated. Among their ranks at that time was one Isander Venizelos. He'd been lured into the movement as a young man with anti-royal, anti-religious sentiments. When Mont Pietat was taken over, he discovered papers revealing the link between the monastery and the Charter. So he set out secretly to find the instructions for locating it. But there was a complication. He had fallen out with the movement, especially after their terrible treatment of the monks killed in the assault. To cut a long story short, he uncovered the Charter's hiding place, but before he could salvage its contents he had to flee in fear for his life, and left the details of the find with a fellow soldier he could trust. This man proved to be worth his weight in gold as he fulfilled the task entrusted to him and was able, in time, to take the Charter down to the coast for safety. That, dear Peredis, is how it came to be in your hands and why it needed to be delivered to Isander Venizelos in the north."

"That's a great story. But what's its value now? Why is it so important still?"

"It's important because it's a contract for freedom which the countries of a free Europa can sign up to. The southern states have already signed. It's the shape of a future society once the tyranny of a federal Europus is taken down and demolished. It's one step nearer your father's goal, Peredis. That's why it's of extraordinary importance."

He stopped here to light his pipe and gently blew a cloud of aromatic smoke into the surrounding air. That aroma was so familiar, Peredis couldn't help smiling for pure pleasure. It took him right back to his childhood and Adhemar's tutorials by the rushing waters of the mountain stream. He had come a long way since then.

At supper that evening, Peredis was able to tell Robert and Adhemar about the amazing sight he had witnessed in the collapse of the royal palace.

"The more you think about it, the more it was inevitable," Adhemar commented. "Technically, the palace, or SEPTIMUS if you will, was unsustainable. It was a ground-breaking piece of technology but beyond the hand of its creators to control. That's my guess. SEPTIMUS started to have his own ideas at some point. It would have happened sooner or later because the system was designed to respond creatively."

"So where does that leave us now?" Robert asked.

"That was my question, too," Peredis echoed. "There's a power vacuum. The royal family have dispersed and scattered who knows where ... Can we take advantage of it? The City itself must be in a state of chaos."

"Yes, we need to find out what happened to the king and the royal family before we can act," Adhemar said.

"There's the question of succession. Who has legitimate power in the absence of the king?"

"Surely it would be the older prince," Robert suggested. "Prince Fion, I believe it is. He's the heir to the throne."

"We need to know if he escaped the collapse," Adhemar said. "And whether he or any of the other royal children have survived."

"And then?" Robert asked.

"And then, go and find him," Adhemar said.

"And who's supposed to do that?" Robert insisted. "And afterwards, do what with him?"

He stopped and looked at Peredis. "Peredis, I suppose," he said. "But why Peredis? Shouldn't he be heading back to Eremore?"

"It's all foreseen, Robert," Adhemar declared. "The end of Europus will come from the old alliance of the Visionaries, but this time united with the crown prince himself. That will make all the difference. And, as you say, it's a job for Peredis."

"And Peredis will go and find the prince and bring him here?"

Adhemar nodded in confirmation. Peredis said nothing. He was thinking of his last conversation with Itxaso. Without her mission to recover the fourfold axe, his role in these events was still only a distant dream. But for the moment, if Adhemar took it for granted that he was the one to search for Prince Fion, he saw no reason to argue with that. On the contrary, he felt that inner thrill again. The call of another great adventure on the horizon.

# Chapter 19

They had to be patient. There was nothing to be done immediately. Peredis sent messages to Vasconia to be forwarded to the City, asking to be kept in touch as soon as fresh developments occurred. In the meantime, he was glad to be home and managing the estate with Robert. Adhemar stayed with them longer, working away at some project of his own in the tower, and it was a delight for Peredis to have his company every evening. They had some excellent conversations during that time on all sorts of topics of which Peredis knew little: forms of government, republicanism, monarchy, democracy, self-determination. He began to see in more depth exactly what it was his father had been fighting for. He also came to realise that in his usual understated way, Adhemar was furthering his education.

News from the City trickled in, and none of it good. There was chaos, as they had suspected would follow the collapse of authority, and a wave of disorder allowed lawless gangs to take over the streets. The gangs battled one another for power and from what they gathered this gave rise to murders and revenge killings so that no one felt safe. They heard lurid stories of wholesale executions and mass graves. Peredis was deeply concerned for Venizelos. Would his guards on the gate be enough to protect him in the event of a raid on his property? The weeks passed and he waited anxiously for news.

When it finally came, news was mixed. Venizelos himself was fine, the worst of the disturbances hadn't affected him, but he was still vulnerable, he said.

As for the royal children, Venizelos thought he knew where two of them were, Prince Fion and his sister Dream. It appeared they might have been taken to a mountain community connected with the Heretics movement, those of the green ribbons. For the moment, then, they were out of danger. Added to which the hill dwellers were completely cut off by snow during the winter months. Peredis had to wait.

And so the weeks passed. But Peredis was getting more and more restless.

Then out of the blue, another message came via the Vasconians. He knew straightaway what it meant.

"The cherries are in blossom."

"That's all?" Robert raised an eyebrow. "What's it supposed to mean?"

"It means the snows have cleared. The way is open for me to go and find the young royals."

"Well, if you say so," Robert had to accept his interpretation but he couldn't disguise his unhappiness. "You've got a long journey ahead of you, then. And no one to go with you this time."

"I'll be fine. I know the route I took with Mikel, and Adhemar always puts protection around me."

"To keep you from harm, Peredis, not to give you permission to do foolish things."

"I think I've grown out of that, Robert."

"I do hope so." He sounded extremely grumpy but Peredis knew it was only because he cared so much. "Make sure you speak to Adhemar, then, before you leave. And pay heed to his every word."

"I will, I promise."

Adhemar was more philosophical about Peredis' departure. "It's meant," was his only comment.

"Any words of advice?"

"Take care when you reach your destination. Not everyone will understand what your purpose is, or why you're there. You'll be a stranger to them and they won't trust you."

"I'll remember. And I'll be careful at all times."

"All will be well," Adhemar said in a serious voice.

Unconsciously Peredis' hand went to the little silver box which his mother had given him and which he always wore around his neck. Those had been her last words to him. "All will be well."

Adhemar nodded meaningfully but said nothing more. So often between them words were simply not needed.

# Chapter 20

On his arrival in the north this time Peredis kept away from the boundaries of the City, despite his curiosity urging him to go nearer and see what conditions there were like. But he decided not to take the risk and stayed within the cover of the forest until he approached the slopes of Venizelos' estate. And it was true – as far as the eye could see, the cherries were in blossom. What a perfect picture of nature in her best clothes!

There were now four guards on the gate. Given the state of the land, Peredis could understand why Venizelos was taking the situation seriously. He could even forgive the guards now if they were a bit tense. But they recognised him straightaway and opened the gate after a quick call to the house. One of them gazed suspiciously at his saddle bags as he passed.

"What a splendid mount you have!" were Sander's first words as Peredis rode up to the house. He came forward to run an appreciative hand through Ximista's mane. "My man will take special care of him, don't worry."

The groom came to lead Ximista away as Sander gazed admiringly after him.

"I keep all my horses in readiness these days," he said. "Life has become very uncertain. You'll have noticed the extra guards on the gate."

"I did," Peredis replied as they walked into the house. "Do you really think you're in danger?"

"Everyone everywhere is in danger, Peredis. And before you ask, yes, I do have enemies, mostly from my republican days. They've never forgiven me for defecting. But I've put measures in place, just in case."

"My tutor Adhemar told me something of your past with the Decadians, and the discovery of the Charter, and ..."

"The whole story would take an entire evening to tell you. And of course it isn't over yet. We're at a critical stage."

At that moment, Maia appeared in the hallway to welcome them. She seemed to have blossomed and

179

grown since Peredis last saw her, and as she came up to Sander and took his arm he realised her relationship with Sander had moved on since his last visit. Now she was very much the lady of the house.

"It's a pleasure to welcome you back." Her smile was warm and sincere.

"It's good to find you all safe and well," he responded.

"And you, too, after your long journey here. I hope it was without incident."

"I kept to the forest and off the main highways. I had a lot of training for that kind of survival during my time in Eremore."

"Eremore, yes, I'm intrigued. For us here it seems a land of magic and mystery, almost unreal. I very much want to hear more. But first you must rest awhile and settle in and we'll meet up later. It might even be warm enough to sit out on the verandah."

The view of the cherry blossom from the porch was truly splendid. A warm spring breeze blew gently from the lower slopes of the orchards and after his journey Peredis allowed himself to bask in the comfort of the surroundings. It was good to see Sander and Maia so at home together, giving each other small signs of affection. She sat close to him and Peredis could see how relaxed he was in her company. He was happy for Sander, for them both, and perhaps, he had to admit, just a bit envious.

"Tell me how things are in the City," he asked. "I was curious and wanted to ride through but thought better of it."

"You were wise," Sander commented. "The City has become a jungle. It was a huge shock for the Federal army when the palace collapsed and the king and queen disappeared along with the royal children. So far the army has remained disciplined and in barracks but I suspect a coup is in the offing. Things can't go on as they are. Everywhere you look there's lawlessness and disorder. Have you heard of the Black Spot?" he asked. Peredis shook his head.

"They're a nasty bunch that's sprung up in the City, hard to say what they believe in except urban terrorism. As far as I can see, they're spoiling for a fight and they don't care who they kill along the way."

"What will you do if it comes to a head?"

"We're ready to go at a moment's notice. In fact, though I don't mean to alarm you, spies are everywhere and your arrival will surely have been noted somewhere down the road. That alone may provoke an attack so we must plan for you to move on as soon as possible."

A troubling thought occurred to Peredis. "Can you trust your guards?"

"I think so, unless someone's paid them off to turn against me. My regulars are faithful, I'm sure, but the extra guards aren't so well known to me."

"Let's hope they can be trusted. Now, I got the message down south that the royal children were hidden away in the mountains. Is that still the case?"

"As far as I know. We believe two of the children, Fion and Dream, were spirited away by some people known as the Heretics to a place called Wildern in the mountains. Of the others we have no news. As you can imagine, the Federals and the Branchists, another royalist movement, are all keen to find Fion, the eldest boy. Anyone who holds the prince can show him to the people and proclaim a new government. It's vital that he's found and protected. The Decadians, if they find him first, will probably string him up in front of the Reform Cathedral. They're die-hard republicans with no love for the monarchy."

"And the Heretics?" asked Peredis. "What kind of people are they? If they're the ones with green ribbons, we saw a number of those in the City being dragged away by some quite nasty-looking men. I felt really sorry for them. What on earth have they done?"

"They want to go back to traditional life, being at one with nature and living at peace with everyone."

"That doesn't sound so bad to me."

"No, I agree, but they hate modern technology, they think SEPTIMUS is the work of the devil and space exploration is an abomination, just a way of repeating elsewhere all the horrors that we're responsible for on this planet."

"I think my uncle Robert would probably go along with most of that."

"There's no place for him in the modern world, then, and least of all in the City."

"I think Robert is perfectly happy where he is," Peredis said with a smile. "But how am I to find Wildern?"

"Jack the Woodsman will guide you there. He knows these mountains and forests like the back of his hand. He'll take you there."

"First I have to find Jack the Woodsman," Peredis laughed.

"No problem. I'll take you to him tomorrow. Will you be ready to travel on after a good night's sleep? We'll get everything prepared tonight so we can move out first thing after breakfast. We'll slip away around the back of the estate so our departure won't be noticed."

Peredis stretched his limbs, still rather stiff from the many days on horseback. His body was yearning for a return to normal comforts after the long trek north. "I'll be ready for anything after a decent sleep in a real bed," he said, "and Ximista will be ready too."

"You have such a handsome horse there," Sander made a face of approval. "Where did you find him?"

"He was a present from my Uncle Robert. He has Arab blood so he's not only handsome but pretty lively."

"You're a lucky man to have such a treasure," Sander said. "My groom will have checked him over after your trip to make sure he's fit." He went on, "What I propose is that you take two horses from the estate as well. If you find the royal children, the time will come to rescue them and you'll need horses for that."

"Sounds good to me," Peredis replied. "That really is planning ahead."

"The best way to avoid problems later," declared Sander. "You'll need good steeds for this mission."

"Now let's go and eat supper before we get into serious horse talk," Maia said, rising to her feet. "I want to know more about that strange and mysterious land called Eremore ..."

# Chapter 21

Peredis couldn't sleep, exhausted though he was. It seemed everything was coming to a climax. He lay awake, alert and wondering. Wildern ... Where had he heard that name before? After a while it came back to him: the Woodsman asking over and over again if we were headed for Wildern. Not Wildern, they'd insisted. Not Wildern. But now it was to be yes, Wildern, yes Wildern. He didn't know why he was feeling so anxious but maybe because this Wildern didn't sound like anything he'd ever known. He felt an unusual sense of danger. He might be travelling in enemy country. Adhemar had said he wouldn't be trusted. Probably, he thought to himself, the suspicion would be mutual.

The house was deathly quiet and Peredis must have nodded off as the fatigue of the journey caught up with him.

He was woken by a hand on his shoulder. It was Sander. He signalled Peredis to be quiet.

"I heard a commotion down at the gate," he whispered. "Get dressed, be ready to leave straightaway. We'll wait for you downstairs and leave by the back door to the stables."

Even as Peredis joined him and Maia in the hallway they heard gunfire coming from the direction of the gate.

"Quick," said Sander and led the way through the back of the house to the stable block. Within minutes they had saddled up their own mounts and the two extra horses which were to accompany Peredis on his mission. They mounted up in the yard, hearing more and more noise coming from the estate driveway. They saw approaching lights flickering behind them as they rode away in the opposite direction, taking a rising path to the upper slopes. The thick blossom on the cherry trees hid their escape as far as the highest ground. Here Sander stopped briefly and looked back. The scene below them, now more and more visible in the dawn light, was dreadful. The house was surrounded by a baying crowd and the torches they carried were already spreading flames through the building.

"The Charter!" I cried, thinking of nothing else at that moment.

Sander's voice was grim. "I put the safe in lockdown before we left. But I'm afraid my house is lost."

"We'll rebuild it, Sander, when this is all over," came Maia's voice full of strength and conviction. He looked towards her and gave her a knowing smile. Then he turned to Peredis. "Do you see what a treasure she is?"

Peredis nodded with a smile. "You're a lucky man, Sander." He grinned. "Let's go." He urged his horse forward and down the slope on the far side. After half a mile or so the track came to woodland and he turned off, taking them into a deep belt of beech trees. The leafy ground between the trees was easy riding and they made good progress until they reached closely planted birchwoods with some undergrowth between them. Here their pace was forced to slacken.

"Not far now," said Sander. "We'll go slowly and with as little noise as possible." He went in front with Maia while Peredis followed up at the rear. Maia and Peredis each led a spare horse. They didn't talk. The atmosphere was too tense and they realised they were still close to danger. Peredis just prayed that Sander's faith in Jack the Woodsman was well founded and that he'd be able to get them safely away.

It wasn't too long before they saw Jack's tower ahead of them. They approached carefully on foot, leading the horses, until Sander gave them a sign to halt while he went ahead. At first Jack was nowhere to be seen but he must have recognised Sander and came out from where he was sheltering. They spoke quietly together until Sander came back to say he'd agreed to guide Peredis once he'd stoked and covered his charcoal mound.

"Maia and I will leave you now," Sander said. "Between you and Jack you'll be able to manage the horses. It's a day's journey and overnight stay to Wildern but there's a bothy where you can sleep, and Jack will take good care of you."

"I can't thank you enough," Peredis gripped Sander's hand in farewell. "And I hate leaving you when you're under attack. I should be fighting for you."

"The time for that will come," he said. Then he reached into his pocket and took out a jagged slip of copper and held it out to him. "This is the key for the lockdown," he said. "I have the other half which fits with yours. When the time comes, we'll rejoin the two halves and retrieve the Charter together from its secure vault. Keep your key safe. The future of Europa will depend on us, after all this is over."

Peredis took his key and put it into a deep pocket. "All this conflict seems so useless," he said, shaking his head in despair.

"That's the tragedy of warfare," Sander said with a sigh. "Pointless destruction, useless waste, hurt and suffering. But we'll do our best to bring it to an end. Once you've played your part with the royal children and brought Fion to our side, we'll join together and put an end to all this senseless barbarity."

Maia came forward to bid Peredis farewell, and took him by surprise as she hugged him warmly.

"Take care," she said. "There's still much danger ahead."

"I'm so sorry about the destruction of your home," he said to them both. "If you're ever in need, come and find me in the south. I will always be there for you."

It was with great sadness that Peredis saw them ride away to what would be an uncertain future. Then he turned back to the task at hand. Jack was scurrying about with split logs which he piled on the smoking mound of charcoal, patching the areas where the fire was becoming too hot.

When he was satisfied with his work, Jack the Woodman looked towards Peredis.

"Wildern?" he asked.

"Wildern."

He took the bridles of the two leading horses and set off at his trotting pace through the trees. He hadn't gone far before he stopped and looked back.

"Venizelos?"

"No," Peredis replied bitterly. "There is no Venizelos now."

"Wildern?" he asked.

"Wildern," said Peredis, "Yes, Wildern." And Peredis followed his path into the forest.

That path would take him on yet another journey. A journey that would decide the fate of many, and bring Peredis closer to his destiny.

# Afterword

It was the day's end, the first day of their long journey. Dream and Fion stood outside on the high terrace of the fortified house, looking north to a horizon lost in distance. In the drawing room behind them, they heard voices, Margaret chatting with Sir Roderick, the laird of Casterfell, and his wife Fiona, who were offering them food and shelter for the night. They were members of the old nobility, lords of this mountainous domain for centuries and, more importantly, secret sympathisers with the Heretics, able to offer a safe house when needed. Their loyalty to the royal family was unquestioned.

Below them valley after valley stretched away, wreathed in low mists. Almost invisible, the faraway crown of the newly created palace pointed upwards from the tree-tops, glimmering white like an opening flower. The old palace, the only world they had ever known, was gone forever, destroyed in the collapse of an unsustainably rigid system. There was no going back.

In the aftermath of the collapse, Fion and his sister Dream chose to follow Margaret, the leader of the Heretics, into her world behind the mountain, and they have no idea of what lies ahead. Who can say if the new world they're travelling to will be more real than what they have left behind? "We create the world we live in," Margaret told them. It seems that is the size of the challenge now before them.

Above the two youngsters, heightened by the dark surroundings of the mountains, there gleam the powdery lights of millions of galaxies which go on forever.

They look up at the starlit sky, tracing the shapes of the constellations their father taught them. "There's so much to be learned from them," he had said. Above all, he had pointed out the seven stars of the Great Bear, circling endlessly around the pole star, the very pivot of the sky, the still centre of the cosmic cycle.

"There!" said Dream, tossing her long blonde hair from her forehead and pointing upwards. "There it is."

Looking upwards at that massive celestial picture, they see the images of all seven, themselves, their parents, their brother Gentil, their sisters Charm and Emerald, appear for a moment, then drift away into dark space. Each of them has set off on their separate journeys. To each their destiny, as yet unknown. "Watch the Bear," their father had repeated constantly in the final days of the old life. It seems there will come a sign.

"Oh, yes," said Fion, almost to himself. "One day, there'll be a sign. One day a time to go back. There's another thing..." he added, glancing at his sister. The chill of the autumn evening is now gathering around them and they turn to go in.

"What's that?"

"Well, all that stuff in the King's Fairy-Tale that we were brought up on ... you know, I always thought it was just a story." He frowned and shook his head sternly as if he had lost all belief.

Dream paused at the door. "I never did," she said in a sure voice.

And they went inside.

Our adventure will continue in the next
installment of the exciting series

# SEVEN SONGS FOR A THRONE

# Behind the Mountain

BY

# C. J. NEYLON